FAMILY AND FRIENDS

ANITA BROOKNER

Hotel du Lac
Look at Me
Providence
The Debut

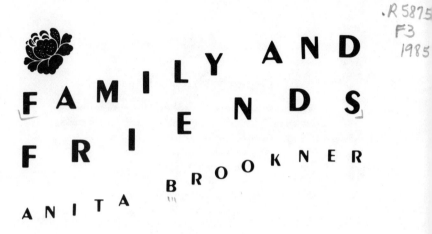

FAMILY AND FRIENDS

ANITA BROOKNER

PANTHEON BOOKS NEW YORK

Library of Congress Cataloging in Publication Data
Brookner, Anita.
Family and friends.
I. Title.
PR6052.R5875F3   1985   823'.914   85-6373
ISBN 0-394-54616-4

Manufactured in the United States of America
First American Edition

THERE IS much to be said for the advantage of rules and regulations, much the same thing as can be said in praise of middle-class society – he who sticks to them will never produce anything that is bad or in poor taste, just as he who lets himself be moulded by law, order and prosperity will never become an intolerable neighbour or a striking scoundrel. On the other hand . . . rules and regulations ruin our true appreciation of nature and our powers to express it.

Goethe, *The Sorrows of Young Werther*, 1774

ONE

H ERE IS SOFKA, in a wedding photograph; at least, I assume it is a wedding, although the bride and groom are absent. Sofka stands straight and stern, her shoulders braced, her head erect in the manner of two generations earlier. She wears a beautiful beaded dress and an egret feather in her hair. It must have been attached to a hat but the hat is hidden by her coiffure, which is in itself hat-shaped. Behind her stand her two daughters, beautiful also, but looking curiously tubercular; perhaps those wide-eyed pleading smiles add to this impression. The daughters are in white, with ribbons in their long hair, which I know to have been red. Sofka's eldest son, her pride and joy, smiles easily, already a lazy conqueror. In his white tie and tails he has the air of an orchestral conductor. He stands between the two girls, an escort rather than a brother, as he was to prove on so many occasions. The sickly and favoured younger son is nowhere in sight, unless he proves to be one of those touching and doomed-looking children seated cross-legged in the front row, the girls, with hair of unimaginable length, clutching posies of flowers, the boys in long trousers and jackets of a satiny-looking material, gazing soulfully at the photographer. Yes, Alfred must be the one on the right. All around them are lesser members of the cast, relations by marriage: a stout and equally beaded woman, several jovial men, a youngish woman with a cascading jabot of lace and an expression of dedicated purpose, and, on the extreme left, edging her way into the centre, a pretty girl with a face like a bird. None of these people seems to have as much right to be in the picture as Sofka does. It is as if she has given birth to the entire brood, but having done so, thinks little of them. This I know to be the case. She gazes out of the photograph, beyond the solicitations of the photographer, her eyes remote and unsmiling, as if contemplating some unique destiny. Compared with her timeless expression, her daughters' pleading smiles already foretell their future. And those favoured sons, who clearly have their mother's blessing, there is something there too that courts disaster. Handsome Frederick, in his white tie and tails, with his orchestral conductor's panache: is there not perhaps something too easy about him, pliable, compliant, weak? Able to engage his mother's collusion in many an amorous escapade, but finally dishonourable, disappointing? Does Sofka already know this? And little Alfred, seated cross-legged between the children who must be sisters and with one of whom he will shortly fall in love, do those eyes, heavy and solemn, shadowed with the strain of behaving well, bear in them the portent of a life spent obeying orders, working hard, being a credit, being a consolation, being a balm for his mother's hurt, a companion in her isolation? For her husband, their father, is absent, gone before, dead, mildly disgraced. Gambling, they say. In any event, he was an older man, scarcely compatible, out of reach to his young children, amused by his young wife but easily bored by her inflexible dignity. Out of it in every sense.

And now I see that it is in fact a wedding photograph. The bride and groom were there all the time, in the centre, as they should be. A good-looking couple. But lifeless, figures from stock. Above the bridegroom's shoulder, standing on something, perhaps, Sofka gazes ahead, with her family's future before her. No one to touch her. As it proved.

I have no doubt that once the photograph was taken, and the wedding group dispersed, the festivities took their normal course. I have no doubt that great quantities of delicious food – things in aspic, things in baskets of spun sugar – were consumed, and that the music struck up and the bride and bridegroom danced, oblivious of their guests, and that the elders gathered in groups on their gilt chairs while the children, flushed with too many sweetmeats and the lure of the polished parquet floor, ventured forth until restrained by nurses or grand-mothers. I have no doubt that as the evening wore on the cigar-scented reminiscences induced many an indulgent nod, a nostalgic smile never to be recovered in the harder commerce of daily life. I have no doubt that those anony-mous and jovial men (husbands, of course) relaxed into the sweetness of this precarious harmony, having found at last what married life had seemed to promise them, and their golden smiles, their passive decent good natures, the sudden look of worldliness their faces assumed as their lips closed voluptuously round the fine Romeo y Julietas and they lifted their heads a little to expel the bluish smoke reminded their wives – censorious women, with higher standards – why they had married them. Sofka would be at the centre of this group, of any group. Handsome Frederick would be dancing, sweeping some girl off her feet, making suggestions which she would not dare take seriously, and perhaps neither would he, with his mother watching him. Later, perhaps, or so the girls would like to think. Little Alfred would manfully trundle his cousin round the floor, looking to his mother for approval, and in so doing lose both her approval and his own heart. The girls, Mireille and Babette (Mimi and Betty), would stay with their mother, waiting for her permission to dance. But the young men, faced with the prospect of negotiating for that permission, would not insist, and the girls would not dance much. Sofka gave out that the girls were delicate. And indeed they looked it.

I find it entirely appropriate and indeed characteristic that Sofka should have named her sons after kings and emperors and her daughters as if they were characters in a musical comedy. Thus were their roles designated for them. The boys were to conquer, and the girls to flirt. If this implies something unfinished, as if the process were omnivorous but static, that too would be characteristic. Sofka sees her children's futures as being implicit in their names, and she has given much thought to the matter; indeed, one wonders whether she thinks about anything else. Her sons, handsome, with the legendary but short-lived handsomeness of those men who die young, are to establish themselves on the ruins of their father's fortune; they are to divide the world and conquer it between them. No matter that Frederick plays the violin so well, and that Alfred is so fond of reading; these accomplishments are for the drawing-room and the study and not for the world. In due course they will lay aside the violin and the books, brace their shoulders, face up to their responsibilities (to Sofka and the girls) and revitalize those factories which have been idle too long. Imperceptibly, they will become tycoons, captains of industry, as their father had been before them. That their father's little weakness – the one he confessed to, that is – might be hereditary Sofka would regard as ridiculous. She repels the thought before it is even formulated. In any event, the boys are so little their father's children; they are, by definition, hers alone. Has she not brought them up single-handed? And are they not a credit to her dedicated mothering? Frederick might break hearts, and he will have her permission to do so. There is nothing the virtuous Sofka admires so much as a man with a bad reputation. Alfred will be encouraged to follow his brother's example; he is too serious by nature and by inclination. See how he clasps his little cousin round her unindented waist and turns his face back to his mother to solicit her smile. And the little cousin already annoyed that his attention should be diverted from her. Better that Alfred should shrug his shoulders and pass on, saving himself, saving them all, from hurt. And he will be even more handsome than his brother when he grows older; he has a soulful poet's face, the ancient eyes of a child prodigy. Alfred is her hope and her investment; he is her second chance. For if Frederick breaks too many hearts to devote much time to the business, that is to say were his career as a boulevardier to interfere with his attendance at the factory, then sad little Alfred, whom Sofka knows to be as serious, as inflexible of purpose as she herself, can be relied upon to assume all the burdens that might otherwise have been shared. With Alfred's help, Sofka knows, she will once again come into her kingdom.

Will the boys marry? Well, of course they will, in so far as everybody marries. But that day might be indefinitely postponed. Sofka does not believe in early marriages; she sees nothing touching in youthful pleasure. She herself had been chosen by a man of substance, well past the age of infatuation. (Or so she believed.) She herself had sought dignity and she thinks that everyone should follow her example. The boys will marry eventually but their brides must be carefully chosen; they will have to be of a suitable pattern to conform with the family destiny. For the family by that stage would once again be rich, very rich. So that extravagant pleasure-loving girls would be out of the question. Sensible women, young enough to produce one or at the most two children, but otherwise fairly mature, and not necessarily very good-looking. Looks are not everything, says beautiful Sofka to her children. And the daughters-in-law will be of a similar background to herself and above all of a similar temperament; thus can Sofka hand on her sons to replicas of herself when she at last, and regretfully, concedes that it is time for them to marry. But that likelihood is in the very distant future, ever more distant as time goes on. In this matter of her sons' marriages, Sofka is inclined to enact both justice and revenge. For if her mothering is to triumph, why should any other woman get the credit? And enjoy the advantage?

And for Mireille and Babette (Mimi and Betty), that time of settling down, as they so wistfully think of it, is so far off as to be almost unimaginable. In the manner of sheltered girls in that unliberated age they long to be married; they long for marriage in order that they might be virtuous young matrons, attentive to their duties and their husbands' welfare, able to supervise servants, and, eventually, the children's nurse. Able to present the bread-winner with evidence of good housewifery, his shirts impeccably laundered and scented with lavender and vetiver, his newspaper and journals intact and uncreased, his house and garden tended, his accounts faultless. Where did they unearth these dreams of innocence? They are beautiful, with a slightly hectic look of which they are probably unaware, and they have been given the names of characters in a musical comedy. And are expected to behave in the same way. For Sofka, that unbending matriarch, young women have a duty to flirt, to engage in heartless and pointless stratagems, to laugh, pretend, tease, have moods, enslave and discard. The purpose of these manoeuvres is to occupy their time, the time that women of a later generation are to give to their careers. By breaking hearts (but never seriously) the girls can give themselves plenty to talk about; they need never be bored, or a burden to their mother. And by keeping a good-natured group of young men in tow ('our crowd') they need never know the grip of a hopeless or unrequited passion and be spared the shame of being left unclaimed. Sofka is quite sincere in determining that her daughters should be spared the humiliation of those who wait. Perhaps she had had this experience herself? Her daughters must be too busy and too light-hearted to tie themselves down; they must laugh and parry even when the proposals are sincere. For there will of course be proposals, from one or other member of the crowd, but the prevailing temper will not encourage the girls to take them seriously. The girls will not want to take them seriously; they will be having too happy a time. Never mind the shirts scented with lavender and vetiver and the uncreased newspapers; there is a new show at the Savoy, and dancing in somebody's house on the river near Henley. And there will always be somebody to bring them home and see that they are taken care of; in any event, they can always rely on their brothers to set a good example in this respect. Marriage? The girls married? Sofka can hardly imagine it, although she has the details of their weddings quite firmly fixed in her mind. There is nothing imaginary about the weddings, only about the whole question of their married lives.

Because there is something about the girls that causes Sofka pain, a soft inward quaking pain. Is it those innocent large eyes, mild and questioning above the coy rouged smiles, that pronounces them unfit for the life their mother has decreed for them, and which she in all her integrity sees as their safeguard? Is there something doomed about those girls, although they are in perfect

13

health and devoted to their mother? What happens to young women, brought up to obedience, and bred to docility and virtue? What happens to such unprotected lives? How will they deal with the world, or the world with them? Sofka sees that her vigilance will be needed to spare the girls the hurt and the shame that even the unsuspecting can endure, even when they are harmless as well as beautiful. When she thinks of the soulful heartless women that she knows, women of her own age, who view the world through narrowed eyes, Sofka feels a hand clutch at her heart. Mimi and Betty, devoted sisters, devoted daughters, brushing each other's long hair at night for all the world as if they were still children, refusing to have it cut, as if they were still little girls. What happens to such daughters? Sofka looks at them sometimes and feels that there is something like a sentence of death on them. Then she determines that they must laugh and flirt and learn all the teasing catchwords, and learn too to disguise the haunting innocence in their large eyes. But all in due course. Let them get used to their social life first. Let them harden naturally. And let them stay with their mother until then. No need to worry too much about partners. The boys can be trusted to bring them home in due course. And once the girls are safe in the bosom of 'our crowd', then Sofka can relax at last.

It was decreed, or it seemed to be decreed, that all the women in that family should have tiny names, diminutives, as if to underline their tiny sparkling natures. The little cousin with whom Alfred is dancing is Nettie (Annette). Somewhere in the background there is a Steffie, and a Carrie. Perhaps the large woman in the photograph is Carrie, a sister-in-law, unaware that she is no longer a diminutive. The husbands refer to these women as 'the girls', having long ago fallen in with the prevailing ideology, always slightly surprised that the girls have grown up and grown older, having met them in the distant past when they all knew each other and formed part of 'our crowd'. Since then they have been subsumed into the matriarchal pattern to which they resigned themselves, without ever knowing what it was. Good-humoured, good-natured, undemanding, unambitious men, chatting over the week's news among themselves until summoned to supply a detail, a compliment, a justification, bidden to rejoin the group. Getting a little stout now, former pleasant looks forgotten, former energy wearing thin. Judged collectively as not quite good enough for the girls, but tolerated, necessary. Golden, indulgent fathers, awakening in their daughters secret dreams of hard fierce brutal men. Fathers of infinite kindliness, easily moved to tears by their children's beauty. Nettie's father is just such a man, easy-going, always smiling. Some would say weak. And Nettie herself will be the sort of child to enslave such a man, with her imperious manners and her arbitrary wishes, apt to fly into a passion and to scream, and have to be taken on to her father's lap and soothed back to happiness. Her mother says that Nettie is 'highly strung', but she understands her perfectly well. Nettie's mother is one of those women who view the world through narrowed eyes. Nettie's mother is possibly the only person in her immediate circle of whom Sofka is slightly afraid.

Sofka herself is a diminutive, of course, although one never thinks of her as in any way diminished, rather the opposite. She is Sophie (Sophie Dorn).

In the photograph the men wear tails or dinner jackets and the women long dresses with little hats, for this is a wedding in the old style, with something of a feeling for the old country. These weddings are important affairs, with the roster of the family's achievements on show. Quiet and retiring as their social lives may be, spent largely in each other's houses, playing cards or discussing the children, with a sharp eye for both perfections and imperfections of housekeeping, the women will prepare for a wedding as if they themselves were getting married. Long sessions with the dressmaker will replace the idle but watchful afternoons in one another's houses, then the shoes, the tiny tapestry bag, and of course the hat will demand all their attention. The children will be indulged with new and impossibly pretty dresses, although these may be a little too young for them. The children will become petulant with the long hours standing in front of a glass, while a dressmaker crawls round them pinning the hem. They do not really like this indoor life, to which they seem to be condemned; it sharpens their nerves and makes them touchy, although they have the beautiful rose-coloured bloom of days spent in the gardens. There are gardens, of course, but they are supervised by gardeners. These days of bustle and calculation will culminate in the actual preparations for the wedding itself. Husbands, cheerfully and with resignation getting into their tails or their dinner jackets, quell an instinctive sinking of the heart as they view their wives' very great solemnity at this moment of their adornment. Iconic and magnificent, the women stand in the centre of their drawing-rooms, and it is difficult to remember that they were ever girls. The children, longing to run and to play, kick moodily around in their enchanting clothes; already they look like men and women, bored with an adult boredom, discontented enough to run for their lives.

Sofka sits in her morning-room, waiting for the car to come round. This is the traditional cry, the view halloo of wedding mornings or afternoons: 'Has the car come round?' Sofka's back is ramrod straight, her beaded dress immaculately appropriate, the hat tiny but triumphal. Around her sit the girls (Mimi and Betty) in their pretty

Pre-Raphaelite dresses, and little Alfred, who is already pale with the heat and the strain. Alfred is always good, but the effort costs him a great deal. Lounging in the doorway, with the nonchalant stance of the Apollo Belvedere, is Frederick who enjoys these long celebrations, offering himself the pleasure of surveying a large field of nubile girls, for weddings put such thoughts into the forefront of every mind. While waiting for the banquet, Frederick is perfectly happy to offer his arm to his mother or his sisters, and indeed is most at home in doing so, for it seems to be his only function within this family. Even now he is pouring his mother a tiny glass of Madeira, placing a small table at her elbow, smiling at her, and very gently teasing her, for she finds these events initially rather daunting. She is a shy woman, virtuous and retiring, caring only for her children, but determined to fulfil her role as duenna, as figurehead, as matriarch. This means presentation, panache, purpose and, in their train, dignity and responsibility; awesome concepts, borne permanently in mind. Like a general on the evening of a great campaign, like an admiral setting a course for his fleet, Sofka looks to the family fortunes and plans her performance accordingly. She surveys her children, is proud of them, trembles for them. The tremor conveys itself to her hand, and a tiny drop of Madeira gleams on the polished wood of the little table. 'Mama,' says little Alfred. 'The car has come round.'

At the wedding they will dance, husbands with wives, fathers with daughters. Under watchful gazes the young people will flirt, amazed that no one is stopping them. The music will become slower, sweeter, as the evening wears on. The children will be flushed, glassy-eyed with tiredness, their beauty extraordinary, as if it were painted. On the gilt chairs the elders will sit and talk. Reflecting, on the following day, Sofka will judge the event a success. Her girls have been congratulated on their charming appearance and manners, her boys on their filial devotion. This is how it should be. Sofka's cheeks have now lost their ivory pallor and her mouth wears a proud smile. In a few days she will receive telephone calls, no doubt with more compliments; she will give one or two tea-parties, for there is much to discuss. The verdicts of those sharp-eyed women, those sisters in the spirit, must be sought, their advice heeded. Strange how much calculation there is even in the most virtuous! Upstairs, in the old nursery, the girls are playing the piano. Little Alfred stands behind his mother's chair until told to go and play. When he receives this permission he hardly knows what to do, for he is rather bad at playing. Frederick, who is very good at it, is nowhere to be seen. Sofka pours coffee, offers cakes. Looking out into her garden, she sees that a wheelbarrow has not been put away. She frowns slightly. How tiresome that so innocent a detail should spoil the perfect picture of her day.

T W O

FREDERICK IS so charming and so attractive that women forgive him his little treacheries. Where others would meet censoriousness Frederick tends to invite collusion. His reputation precedes him, for that is reputation's only useful function. In this, perhaps, he finds the justification for his behaviour. He can never understand what is wrong when people upbraid him. When the occasional woman screams at him, accusing him of forgetting his promise to take her somewhere, or saying that he was reported to have been at that same somewhere with somebody else, Frederick shakes his head, bemused. Frederick does not, in his own estimation, break promises; he merely forgets them. 'You know what a hopeless memory I've got,' he smiles, tapping his marble forehead with his poetic hand. 'You know what I'm like,' he smiles, deep into the woman's eyes. At such relentless and hypnotic persuasion the reproachful woman falters. She tries to retrieve the situation by exacting from him another engagement, half aware that she is on a doom-laden course. It is important to her to be seen in public with Frederick, but as time passes this is not so easy to arrange as it used to be. Whole edifices of status are built on this sort of public appearance, reputations salvaged or lost. Somewhere she is conscious of the fact that the women in Frederick's life are either all equally important or all equally unimportant. Perhaps his reputation has taken over his behaviour. Misgivings increase. Is it better never to make a fuss? What must one do to encourage Frederick's affection once one has lost that turn of the head that proclaims his interest? Does one laugh, give in to him, go along with his little dishonesties? Or does one, once and for all, fling down the gauntlet? How much attention should one pay to the knowledge that if one does engage in this sort of flinging one is likely to live in permanent exile from Frederick and his kind? 'Neurotic,' shrugs Frederick, and his cronies agree. Some of them women.

The exiled woman has been heard to remark that if Frederick behaves in this manner it is because his mother has encouraged him, that it was in fact Frederick's mother who first gave him licence to misbehave at all. Frederick's mother would, if she had ever heard it, react to this opinion with genuine amazement. Is it her fault, she might ask this hypothetical critic, if her elder son has inherited his father's legendary way with women? This is a clever but uncalculated statement, in the way of all Sofka's statements. In the first place it establishes the legend of a heroic line of charming and handsome men, the sort of men who make women conscious for the first time of their powerlessness. In the second place it establishes the superior power of Sofka herself, able to finesse this potent charmer into marriage. None of this is entirely true, of course; the commerce between the sexes is rarely so simple or so just. But the function of such an argument is to annul the criticism of the disappointed, the rancorous, the deceived. Sofka implies that there is little that women can do about such men. A look of distaste crosses her face as she contemplates the possibility of effort, of stratagem, of reproach. Sofka is such a lady, and such a mother. Her husband, the reprobate, almost vanished into thin air after he married her. Fortunately, his reputation was still there to sustain him. In the same way, his reputation now sustains Sofka. And if she looks with an indulgent eye on Frederick, it is because she sees in him his father's disgraceful charm. And a mother is more susceptible to this sort of charm than a wife or a lover can ever be.

When the telephone rings, and Frederick fears an importunate voice, he signals to his mother, and she gets up from her chair with the most extraordinary expression of girlish glee on her face. 'I'm afraid Frederick is out,' she will say in her soft grave voice, one hand to her mouth to subdue her smile. The voice continues in her ear, becoming plangent, and clearly audible to Frederick on the other side of the room, one hand wearily marking time to the reproaches. Sometimes, when Sofka is unable to terminate the conversation as briefly as decency tells her is necessary, Frederick sets his metronome going and his mother is obliged to bring her handkerchief up to her mouth to stifle a little laugh. Sofka loves this teasing relationship with her son and sees no reason why she should forgo it. It brings a little light-heartedness into her serious grown-up life. It makes her feel like a girl again. And no harm is meant by it. Harm may be done, but it is never meant.

Sometimes Sofka will wait up for Frederick when he has been out in the evening. She will prepare a jug of iced lemonade and wait for him in the morning-room, sitting peacefully in the light of one shaded lamp. She looks very charming in repose. To Frederick she is an oasis of sanity in a world peopled by increasingly difficult women. He sighs thankfully when he reaches this haven, and after kissing his mother flings himself into a chair and allows Sofka to pour him a glass of lemonade. Sofka will often have a little embroidery to hand on these occasions: she somehow judges it necessary not to look at Frederick in order to facilitate his confidences. Frederick is rueful, Sofka is smiling. It is the smile of a woman who understands men. Sofka does not know that women who understand men are unreliable allies. Her only allegiance is to her family, so the question does not arise. Sofka can see that something is wrong; her probing is almost imperceptible. Yes, says Frederick, he is rather tired. The evening had not been guaranteed to relax him. Why do women make fusses? In this way he rationalizes his delayed arrival, his straying attention, his glad recognition, across the space of the restaurant, of another girl. Tears, of course, in the taxi. Sofka smiles into her embroidery. 'I can't face her again tomorrow,' says Frederick, assuming an expression of great nobility and weariness. 'There's only so much I can do for her. I can't be expected to deal with her problems. I doubt if anyone could.' Sofka agrees. When the girl telephones in the morning, Sofka will say that Frederick is out and that she does not know when to expect him back. This patent untruth will sometimes bring a girl to the house, in tears. 'My dear,' sighs Sofka. 'I wanted to spare you.' So delicate is Sofka's treatment on these occasions that the girl is quite puzzled to realize that she feels no resentment.

Frederick's deportment, in love and business, is extremely aristocratic. Somehow, out of the unpromising debris of a European family, Sofka has bred an English aristocrat. This is perhaps her most triumphant achievement. Frederick's looks, his smiling dismissal of his small but genuine musical gift, and his ability to treat work as play confirm his unassailable lack of effortfulness. At the factory, which is largely run by the works manager, a hardheaded and devoted German who knew Sofka's husband in the old days and who was in fact previously employed by him as a major-domo, Frederick charms everyone, employees, clients, secretaries, machine minders.

They never know when he is coming in, and so they work harder: the uncertainty, and the desire to earn one of his winning smiles, makes them all very conscientious. There are as yet no partners but a place is being kept for Alfred, who will start there – at the bottom, of course – as soon as his schooling is finished. Never mind the studies and the books and the growing obsession that Alfred has with distant places: he must work first and earn the right to play afterwards. But Frederick seems to play all the time; he is the original *homo ludens*. He will often arrive in his office in the early afternoon, having let the whole morning go to waste. Sometimes he will be carrying golf clubs, a tennis racquet, for one of the delightful things about Frederick is his imperturbability. A weak man might invent excuses but Frederick, with the knowledge that he is the family's pride and joy and an object of scandal and desire, will not bother to be anything but himself. Perhaps a client has been waiting for him for some time and is getting restive; clients, after all, are not necessarily under Frederick's spell. But Frederick will wave such a person into his office, make a comic face behind his back to his secretary, and in his charming way, which the client considers extremely European, offer him coffee and iced water and cigars. For brief periods Frederick can manage to be an enthusiast, and it is this lightning enthusiasm, apt to fade very fast, that tends to attract investment. Besides, Frederick's very outrageousness is entertaining. Here too his reputation has preceded him. It seems quite an achievement to have gained his attention for as long as half an hour.

With the astonishing luck that is somehow coaxed out of circumstances by impudent behaviour, Frederick has managed to put the factory on its feet. This is the reputation that Frederick is allowed to have, although the steady work is done by Lautner, the ex-major-domo, who, having only a cramped and unattractive flat to go home to, is there at all hours. Lautner sometimes sleeps at the factory if he has been working late on an order, or going through the figures. He is not above brushing Frederick's lapels before he leaves the office. With Lautner there nothing is left to chance, and he is so devoted to the family and his days and nights are so devoid of entertainment that the factory is his life. Lautner, in fact, should be a partner, but it would be unkind to demote him when Alfred finally makes it to the top. Although Alfred is only sixteen, his rise to managerial importance is discussed as if it will come about in a matter of months. When these discussions take place Alfred hangs his head so that his mother should not see the dark expression which he has never been able to hide; in due course he invariably slips out of the room and goes back to *The Conquest of Peru*. Frederick is quite understanding about this and cuffs him affectionately round the head, but there is no question of Alfred's course in life being changed. Home is such an agreeable place, and Sofka so delicate a mother. And the money is beginning to return and life is easier and very pleasant. There is Elizabeth in the kitchen and Winnie who comes in every day to do the rough work, and the dressmaker and the hairdresser now come to the house again. The chauffeur is paid two pounds a week. Sofka is able to indulge her little weakness again: beautiful monogrammed linen. The children are encouraged to give her fine white embroidered lawn handkerchiefs as presents, but dashing Frederick will turn up with a bouquet of flowers and Sofka will forget the other little tributes. Sometimes Frederick will present his mother with one red rose. There are roses in the garden, of course, but they are the province of the gardeners. Frederick's rose will be placed in a vase and taken up to Sofka's bed-table. As she lies back on the square pillows that her mother

24

gave her when she married, Sofka will look at the rose and smile.

In this world of weddings and marriages Frederick is the dark horse, the enigma. He is also the trump card. Who will win Frederick? The contestants are many, and their fight for the conquest of his hand has begun to contain elements of panic and disappointment. Sofka has always encouraged her children to bring their friends to the house, but only Frederick avails himself of this offer. He loves his friends to meet his mother and they are encouraged to come to tea on Sunday afternoons. In this way more than one aspirant has found herself face to face with someone rumoured to be a rival, for rumour thrives on this sort of confrontation. Frederick and his mother see nothing shaky in this arrangement; indeed, Sofka thinks it redounds to Frederick's credit that he openly shows his hand. The sheer good manners demanded by the pleasant worldliness of these occasions subdue sharp reactions, and looks of dismay are turned into agreeable and sophisticated smiles. Sofka, who loves Sunday afternoons, puts herself out to entertain the girls. They are shown the garden, rather slowly, and asked if they would like to sit out there for a little while. Frederick, who remains in the drawing-room, allows his mother to do the honours. Then there is tea, with Frederick's favourite marzipan cake. 'Freddy, you'll get fat,' shriek the girls, half-hoping that he will. 'Freddy?' smiles Sofka. 'Is that what you call him?' She implies a very slight lowering of standards here, which would not be tolerated in her own family. The girls attempt to salvage something from what is already perceived as a missed chance by being extraordinarily nice to Mimi and Betty. Mimi is so charming, so like her mother: why do the girls prefer Mimi? If she is like her mother, she is also unlike her mother, but it is difficult to tell how, and there is so much more to think about than this little matter. The struggle for control becomes more arduous. No sooner does one of the girls decide to make a positive move by asking Frederick to take her home and thus, at last, getting him on his own, than Sofka says, 'We always enjoy a little music on Sunday afternoons,' and bids Frederick take up his violin. With Mimi at the piano, there follows an interminable arrangement of something or other which entails rapt attention and minimal movement. When Frederick at last lowers his violin and Mimi strikes her final chord, the girls are so relieved that their applause is genuinely enthusiastic. Mimi flushes becomingly but Betty seems already to be completely aware of what is going on. When the girls get up to leave, there being no other ploy available, Sofka shakes their hands kindly. 'I'm so glad you enjoyed our little concert. You must come again some time,' she says. 'I want to meet all Frederick's friends.' She implies that their number is legion and that they are all female. Both implications are correct.

Having disheartened so many women, Frederick can hardly complain if they marry the nearest man to hand, as indeed they tend to do. He views these weddings, which he enjoys, with an indulgent eye, sizing up the bridegroom with a sense of genuine camaraderie. As he dances, in his white tie and tails, only slightly fuller in the face and figure than he was at that earlier wedding in the photograph, he feels renewed affection for the bride. Soon he will take to calling on these married women, with whom he maintains a teasing relationship, and is amazed to find them so tart of tongue. 'Has marriage made you cynical?' he murmurs, looking into their eyes with his famous smile. And, 'I feel I'm really getting to know you for the very first time,' he says, reluctantly relinquishing a hand. It is his best exit line. Is he aware that he is becoming rather well known for it? He shrugs.

What of it? Frederick has always worn his misdemeanours on his sleeve. It has served to make him unassailable. And what is really touching is that so many of these young matrons have learnt to make marzipan cake, creating for Frederick little homes away from home. This suits Frederick, that favourite son, very well indeed. Sometimes he finds himself automatically flirting with his mother. But then he always has.

Husbands view him with something like condescension. He is the *Hausfreund*, the wife's companion, the husband's ally; he can be trusted. He is now too lazy and too spoilt to do much more than make intimate conversation. Sometimes he feels a twist of boredom, pats down a yawn. But most of all he feels that he has done well, both for himself and for his family. By family he means his mother. He has not abandoned her for another woman. He has maintained the household on its course. The girls will be well provided for, and Alfred, though silent on the matter, has acknowledged that he will enter the factory after the summer holidays. This suits Frederick very well, because business is beginning to bore him too. He leaves so much to Lautner that he rarely needs to be in his office. And Lautner is so serious and so dedicated that he sometimes calls round on a Sunday evening to discuss the coming week's affairs with Frederick, so as to spare him undue attendance. Sofka is very pleasant to Lautner, whose punctilious good manners she appreciates. He kisses Sofka's hand, is bidden to sit down, and is given hot coffee and any marzipan cake that happens to be left over. 'Well, Mr Lautner, I will leave you with my son,' she murmurs, when he is halfway through his coffee. Lautner remains standing, his little linen napkin in his hand, until Sofka has left the room. Lautner can no longer bear to think of Sunday without his coffee and cake in Sofka's drawing-room. He would walk there and back if he had to. He is, as Frederick and Sofka both know, devoted to the family. They hope that Alfred will soon shake off that rather surly expression and buckle down to work. Once he is under Lautner's eye, they all think, he is bound to do well. The girls peer over the stairwell. 'Good-night, Mr Lautner,' they call. He looks up, startled and delighted. Betty immediately retreats with a giggle, but Mimi, blushing for her sister, forces herself to remain, and waves a hand in compensation.

So Frederick hardly bothers to go to the factory, having lost that faculty of instant, whiplash enthusiasm that won the firm so many orders. But this does not matter very much, for they now have everything they want, and the name is established. It is left to the painstaking Lautner to try to charm the buyers, and this he singularly fails to do, but at the same time he is so rigorously honest that they shrug and renew the order anyway, knowing that their money is safe. The only difference is that nobody works quite so hard as they did in the days of Frederick's brief suzerainty. The old enthusiasm, the old feeling for the place is gone. Lautner mentions this to Frederick who is not altogether displeased to hear it. He looks to Alfred now to compensate for his own vanished charm with a lifetime of unstinting toil.

On the whole, life is very pleasant, very comfortable. In her drawing-room, lightly touching the roses brought in that morning by the gardener, Sofka smiles, listens, sits contented. Being a lady, she does very little, but her house is well run, as it should be, her monogrammed linen immaculate, and the soft sweet food that she prefers always lavish. Above her head the girls, Mimi and Betty, practise their scales. Betty has developed a very good singing voice, and sometimes Mimi accompanies her in a performance of Massenet's 'Elégie' ('O doux printemps *d'autrefois . . .'*) which is too old for her. All the songs that Betty favours are too old for her, just as her clothes are too young; there is something about Betty that is impatient to discard the clothes and investigate the songs. It is Mimi, the serious one, who conscientiously rips through the accompaniment of *'Les Filles de Cadiz'*, which her sister sings with many a haughty glance and a smouldering expression, both directed at the walls of the old nursery. Sofka, who does not see the glances, because she is not looking for them, hears only the refracted melody, and, in her drawing-room, gently beats time with her hand. When she next has a tea-party for Carrie and Steffie and Letty, and when their husbands, Max, Sam, Dizzy (Desmond), come to collect them and sit down briefly to enjoy a glass of schnapps, Sofka will ask the girls to perform one of their duets on the drawing-room piano. *'Les Filles de Cadiz'* comes to be their party piece, although Betty's performance leaves one of the visitors with a tiny doubt in his mind. Carrie, too, that redoubtable matron, looks thoughtful, but being of the same immaculate presentation as Sofka herself, preserves a gracious expression.

All this time Alfred is in his room, using his remaining hours of leisure to cram in as many books as possible. He dreams of a vast library, kept under lock and key, for his own private use. So anxious is he that this domain must be safely guarded that he sometimes denies that he has been reading at all, when his mother lays a hand to his hot brow. 'I was thinking about next year at the factory,' Alfred tells her, and this is not altogether a lie, since the factory is what he most dreads and fears. He does not know that when he starts at the factory he will inherit power, and that means power to buy books. It seems to him, or would do, if anybody ever bothered to explain it to him, such a complicated and uninteresting manipulation of access to the printed word. Reading, to Alfred, means his cool back bedroom at home, with a curtain blowing in front of the open window, and a white counterpane on his soft bed and his dead father's desk in the corner, waiting to be made his own. Reading, for Alfred, means a dream of home that he is condemned to lose, to forfeit, in some unsought trial of manhood. Reading means his sister's voice drifting up the stairs and the polite clapping of the visitors and the faint chink of coffee-cups. Reading means Mimi knocking at his door and handing in a glistening slice of cherry tart. Only Mimi bothers to knock. For this, Alfred loves her best. His mother must never know this.

And Frederick, as time passes? Frederick has discussed so many women with his mother that he has betrayed them all. Frederick sits where Sofka has always wanted him to sit, opposite her, in the chair her husband once and briefly occupied. Frederick has filled out considerably: he is now violin shaped, and his beautiful face has the ruined charm of a professional voluptuary. This adds to his attraction in the eyes of some, but not of all. He is beginning imperceptibly to resemble those cheerful husbands (Max, Sam, Dizzy), those stalwarts of 'our crowd', those fundamentally decent men who never pass judgment. Why should they? They know, these men, that they are aliens, whatever airs their wives give themselves. They retain, from some anterior life, caution, prudence, an awareness of possible danger. And besides, they never thought that Frederick had any harm in him. They never thought that he went too far, or indeed went far enough. Without his reputation, Frederick is indeed an amiable, some might say a harmless, figure. And he is such a good son, such a joy to his mother. And he has done so well for them all. This early effort of Frederick's will be resurrected from time to time when circumstances change. 'He has done so well for us all,' smiles Sofka, resting a loving hand on her son's arm. 'And he did so well for them all,' the men will ruefully remark, shaking their heads, in later years, when Frederick, absent, sits in the bar of an hotel on the Riviera, and, once more, lays himself out to please.

T H R E E

I F ANYONE HAD ever bothered to tell her, Betty would
know that she bears a marked resemblance to Colette,
that redoubtable French writer of whom Betty has never
heard. She has the same mat of red hair, uncut, closely
waved, altogether excessive in its length and thickness;
the same cat's eyes, long and narrow; the same sharp
puckered mouth. Her appearance, which has acquired an
edge entirely missing from her sister's more tranquil,
more unfocused beauty, could have been memorable
were it not for a spark of calculation in the eyes and a
tendency for the mouth to remain in a studied moue
while the glance ranges thoughtfully above. Her beauty,
therefore, approximates more to prettiness than it would
otherwise have done had it been warmed into reflection,
or coloured by memory. Betty is good-natured rather
than kind. At fifteen she is already the accomplished flirt
that her mother has always thought she wanted her to be.
Plump and petite like Sofka, with the same small hands
and feet, Betty has a guttersnipe charm. 'Elle a du chien,'
murmured the women admiringly among themselves when
Betty, as a child, swept into an elaborate curtsy, with an
adorable lift and fall of the shoulders. The women are more
innocent than Betty, who has already outgrown her tender
dreams of married bliss, and has decided to run away from
home and become a dancer at the Folies-Bergères.

Betty has long since given up the languorous and mutual ritual of hair brushing, that innocent activity in which the girls dream of their tender future; her thoughts are now sharper and are couched in the first person singular. Privately she turns her attention to the décor of her mother's house which she finds stuffy and lacking in style. Those brown velvet sofas, those *portières*, always absorbing sunlight and smelling of pepper, those mahogany wardrobes, those high beds with their carved headboards and their feather eiderdowns, those sideboards, that long ancestral dining table – all this she would sweep away. She would replace them with something lighter and more modern, in tones of green and orange, with plenty of glass and white paint. The only thing she would retain from Sofka's life is that little cabinet filled with fans. And those dreadful silk foulard dresses that Sofka wears, her white silk blouses and collars with the little bar brooch at the neck, these would have to go too. Betty sees her mother, or, if her mother will not consent, herself (and this is even less likely) in patterned georgette cut on the bias and a georgette handkerchief slipped through an ivory bracelet worn high on the left forearm. Until she can put these revolutionary plans into operation she involves Mimi in the serious business of trying on their clothes; she has arranged to exchange her pinks and blues with Mimi's navy and grey, for Mimi is older and is therefore allowed these grown-up colours. On Betty they look arresting and mildly inappropriate; her word for them is chic, although she frowns at the high necklines and is already busy on the collars. Fortunately she is good with her needle and therefore always looks better than Mimi who is not. Mimi remains dreamy and mild, is content with her long hair, and practises the piano far more than she need.

It is in fact Mimi's piano that allows Betty access to that

outside world for which she is so ardently prepared. Once a week she accompanies Mimi to her lesson with Mr Cariani in Marylebone Lane. Mr Cariani is an entirely correct and middle-aged man of vaguely Sardinian parentage whose small and select academy houses two music rooms and a studio for Greek dance which is thought to be of benefit to girls suffering from round shoulders. These girls, a disconsolate group, assemble once a week and go through their movements to the resounding rhythms and uplifting exhortations of Miss Mudie, who plays the piano. The thumping and somehow defeated noises made by these girls drift through the ceiling to the music room above, where Mr Cariani attempts to guide Mimi through a Chopin prelude. As the sweet painful harmonies take shape under Mimi's fingers, Betty, seeing her sister's attention relaxing into absorption and Mr Cariani smiling as he leans over Mimi's shoulder, lifts her pointed chin questioningly, lets her eyes rove round the room, and fixes her gaze on the door through which, sooner or later, Mr Cariani's son Frank (Franco) will appear.

Mimi, in her innocence, is merely aware of her sister's impatience on these occasions and has no difficulty in ascribing it to her own concentration on her music to the detriment of all other talents to amuse. Mimi always has a vague sense of guilt when she is not entertaining people, for Sofka has told her that she should be known for her high spirits if she wants to be popular. Mimi feels doubly guilty when her sister manifests annoyance for she knows that Betty possesses those ideal and unattainable high spirits which her mother has enjoined upon her. Betty has already been agitating on her seat in the bus, anxious to catch a glimpse of her profile reflected in the glass of the window, and on arrival at Mr Cariani's has twitched up her skirt to smooth her stockings, running her hand voluptuously along the inside of her calf and above the knee to her thigh. 'Betty!' says Mimi, shocked. 'Behave yourself. What if Mr Cariani's son were to see you?' But Betty takes her time. It is after all for the benefit of Mr Cariani's son that the performance with the stockings is being enacted.

Although Sofka has paid a formal visit to Mr Cariani before entrusting the girls to his weekly tuition and has found him entirely deferential, satisfactory, and known to other mothers in her circle, she is not aware of the existence of Mr Cariani's son. This is just as well, for Mr Cariani's son is perhaps destined to make Sofka withdraw Mimi and Betty from his disturbing presence. Frank Cariani is a throwback to some Sardinian shepherd who may just conceivably have engendered the entire Cariani line. He is dark, lithe, dangerously handsome; he is in addition both sulky and shy. In his white shirt, black trousers and black pumps, he looks like a wild creature whose nakedness is struggling to dominate his unaccustomed trappings. He is in fact quite a good fellow, quite decent, but his father senses in him an animal quality which it pains him to see in the general setting of the music that is practised in his studio. For some months now Frank has been begging his father to allow him to conduct lessons in various character dances when the Greek girls are not mournfully monopolizing the downstairs room. Miss Mudie, unexpectedly, is all for it. She is sick of playing Grieg over and over again. That is how Frank's classes in the tango, the rumba and the cachucha have brought large numbers of pupils and mild prosperity to Mr Cariani's establishment. That is how Betty comes to be in Frank Cariani's arms, bent back as if in a swoon, her thick plait touching the floor, her face rapt and mysterious, before swinging upright and with sharp and angular movements of her head and shoulders retrieving her ascendancy over her handsome partner.

35

There is no doubt that they are both extremely gifted. Frank dances quite simply, as if that was what he was born to do, but Betty is altogether more disturbing. Betty compresses her mouth, narrows her eyes, and stamps her feet as if she were in the grip of some erotically-charged bad mood. Whereas Frank moves easily and naturally, Betty seems to obey some inner tangle of tensions and energies. These are apparent in the way she stretches her neck and ripples her shoulders, points and withdraws her foot, snaps her fingers. Gradually Frank accepts that his perfect and unemphatic movements are merely a foil for Betty's more complex attitudes. Betty is a good dancer but she is a much better actress. She is acting the part of a passionate and scornful woman of Mediterranean habits and lineage, whereas she is in fact the milky-complexioned child of reclusive Europeans. As she strives to adapt her virgin body and her complicated and corrupt temperament to the Latin steps, her face takes on the precise and moody urgency of a Parisian artist's model.

There is indeed something Bohemian about Betty although to all intents and purposes she has never been far from her mother's house. Sofka has noted this quality and has decided that although Betty's temperament was quite amusing in a little girl, promising those admired high spirits later on in life, it must now be supervised, rigorously controlled, and if necessary corrected. Sofka loves Betty's fire, admires her looks but feels estranged from that perverse spirit that has always inclined Betty to moods, sulks, and screaming tantrums. She no longer screams these days, having found more subtle and effective ways of imposing herself. She will seem to withdraw her love, her admiration, her loyalty, and will be seen quite clearly to calculate her own as against her family's chances of success. Consequently people will make more of an effort to win Betty's good opinion and consent than if she were polite and well behaved. Sofka is also rather unpleasantly aware of Betty's altogether unwelcome sexuality. Of all her children Betty appears to be almost viciously in touch with her own lower instincts, and although nothing has prepared her for life in the adult world (Sofka has seen to this) she is clearly ready to test her powers on any man who might come within range. She always flirted as a little girl with those kindly uncles, and now that she is no longer a little girl she does not bother to do so; this apparent withdrawal of favour bewilders the uncles who cry, 'No kiss for me today?' in a hurt tone which quite displeases Sofka. And there has been a regrettable incident, the last in a series of several, when Sofka, on entering the girls' bedroom, has found Betty trying on one of her own nightgowns, a simple voile shift in the colour known as '*Nuage*', which Sofka had made for a certain holiday she took with her husband in Baden-Baden. Not only has Betty taken it out of Sofka's chest of drawers; she is peering at the piquant little body which it reveals, well aware that she is more finely made than her mother. Sofka and Betty both see this at the same time. And that nightgown has not been worn since Sofka's husband, the reprobate, died. The conjunction of all these reflections has given Sofka a sense of grievance which is periodically mobilized into a headache, for nothing on this earth would permit Sofka to brood on certain aspects of her long and respectable widowhood.

Now Betty is demanding that Sofka allow her to have her hair cut. That beautiful hair! Sofka regards the girls' hair as being in the nature of her own possession, something that she will hand over like a sacred torch to whomever shall claim the girls in marriage. After that they can do what they like with it, although Sofka will always hark back with a reminiscent smile to its earlier glory.

Sofka would like the girls to remain as children while they are in her care. This is, after all, only good form. Their thoughts and attitudes, if they have any – and Sofka does not see this as necessary – they must keep to themselves. It is the least they can do. Mimi shows every sign of conforming to this unwritten and indeed unspoken rule. Mimi is the girl that Sofka has always decided she should be, staid, enchanting, and naïve. Mimi's presence in a room is registered, but not entirely noticed. Betty is a different matter altogether.

This business of the hair has been discussed, with slightly raised voices, many times. The boys have been called in to back up Sofka's refusal. Frederick has not been entirely helpful. He tugged at Betty's plait, and said, 'If you only knew how much naughtier you look like this,' at which both Betty and Sofka gave him a sharp glance, only to meet his ruefully innocent gaze. But Alfred is furious. Alfred, like Mimi, is pure, with a scornful purity that resists all advances. 'Of course you can't have it cut,' he shouts. 'Why can't you wait until you're grown up?' Alfred has surrendered his own childhood so unwillingly that he cannot understand how anyone could want to get rid of such a beautiful commodity. 'I am grown up,' screams Betty, reverting to an earlier pattern. At which Sofka intervenes in genuine distaste. A scene in her own drawing-room is something she will never permit. She sends Betty and Alfred to their rooms and the whole question is shelved. So effectively is it shelved that Sofka can hardly complain, or so Betty maintains, when Betty returns one afternoon from Marylebone Lane with her hair shorn into a bushy triangular bob, looking more like Colette than ever.

Sofka is genuinely heartbroken. She sits down in her chair and weeps, so brokenly that even Betty is uncomfortable. Betty, in one of those brief changes of mood that are to make her irresistible, kneels down by her mother's chair, covers her hand with kisses, and weeps just as brokenly as Sofka; more so, perhaps, for her sobs are intermingled with cries of 'Mama! Mama! Talk to me!' Sofka raises haggard eyes from her handkerchief and, seeing her daughter a little girl again, bends forward to comfort her. The boys are uneasy, Frederick mildly sorry that this had to happen, and Alfred struggling over a decision never to speak to Betty again. With a desolate light dawning in her eyes, Sofka turns to Mimi. 'You were with her. She is your little sister. You are supposed to take care of her. Why did you let her do this?' She speaks as though Betty has sustained some terrible injury. So genuine is her grief that Mimi hardly likes to explain that Betty had slipped out of the studio while she was performing her Chopin *étude* and, guided by Frank, had commanded the nearest Italian barber to cut off her hair. Mimi would feel disloyal if she said any of this. And so the matter is laid to rest, with Sofka and Betty reconciled, and a slight animus against Mimi. The next day, Sofka telephones M. Emile, her own hairdresser, to come to the house and even up Betty's hair. Within a few days Betty is all smiles, having got her own way. 'Not bad,' concedes Frederick. 'Not bad at all.'

But of course this will not satisfy her for long, and Sofka wonders what will happen when she comes into her own money. It was decreed by their father that the girls should receive one thousand pounds each on the day that the younger reaches her eighteenth birthday. In that way there will be no envy, no rivalry. It is one of his few sensible decisions, the last he made before his relatively early demise which is usually accredited to his lavish private life and seigneurial business practices. Sofka does not have too long to wait before she finds out. On the fateful day, which happens to coincide with one of their weekly visits to Mr Cariani's, the girls arrive home at tea-time. Mimi has celebrated by buying her mother a large bunch of flowers. 'Silly girl,' says Sofka, smiling. 'My silly girl. We have so many in the garden.' But she takes the lovely roses and for a moment, as she looks down at them, she has to bite her lip to quell a dangerous pang of emotion. It is not the gesture that moves her so much as the spectacle of Mimi's simplicity. Mimi is now twenty years old, her second child, and yet she behaves as if she were fifteen. So sweet, so docile: how can such goodness survive, and who will claim it? How will Mimi know who is worthy of her? How will she fare when her mother is no longer there to guide her?

She need have no such fears for Betty. Betty is celebrating by paying renewed attention to her appearance. During her attendance at Marylebone Lane Betty has taken advantage of the piano lessons and has made a tour of the nearby stores. She has returned with numerous pairs of flesh-coloured stockings, a new dress patterned with spiders' webs of white on a navy ground, some red beads and matching bracelets, and some extremely high-heeled shoes. With this outfit, in which she looks years older than Mimi, she wears a great deal of kohl shadow on her eyelids, while her upper lip, rouged in a sharply pointed bow of Indian red, lifts slightly over her small white teeth. The weight of the shadow on her lids makes her narrow her eyes. She has also started smoking, with so little difficulty that it is impossible to believe that she has not been doing so for some time. With the ivory cigarette-holder between her teeth and her fingernails painted bright red, with her legs crossed high, her brooding eyes and her sharp teeth, Betty looks like a painting by Foujita, a native Parisian, a Bohemian, a fallen angel.

There is something about Betty's new appearance that is so complete, so utterly thought out that, unlike her hair, it leaves no room for modification. This gives Sofka pause. Here is the intimation of a work of art and she is quick to appreciate it. But she is also quick to see that it has been created not for her approval but to court opposition. This she withholds, merely laughing gently and touching Betty's necklace in passing as if amused by so much artificiality. Sofka is extremely practised in these arts, which she expects from every other woman. Sofka hardly believes in the solidarity of her sex unless it is united by bonds of mutual standing: sisterhood, matrimonial status, mother love. She is well aware that Betty is one of those women, rather like herself, in fact, who is the instinctive ally of men. Gentle amusement, the lightest of touches, the merest flutter of surprise, are all that Sofka will permit herself in the course of this particularly feminine commerce. But she has it in her to fear for Mimi, who will not profit from close companionship with her sister, and will not learn from it either, and for whose sake it might be politic to separate the two girls. Sofka thinks of that little cousin, Nettie, of whom Alfred used to be so fond. So temperamental did Nettie prove to be that her mother, Carrie, had to send her to a finishing school in Switzerland to have her bad manners shamed out of her by other, more scornful girls. It might not be a bad idea, thinks Sofka, to send Betty to join her cousin in Switzerland for a while. This is under active discussion.

It is quite clear that Betty will have to go somewhere. Even Mimi is vaguely troubled by those high spirits which Betty chooses to manifest in public. The girls have taken to having afternoon tea at a *pâtisserie* in town after their lesson and on these occasions Betty reveals herself as being very high-spirited indeed. 'Don't look round,' she hisses to Mimi. 'Move your chair closer to mine. There's a man over there who can't take his eyes off me.' 'Where?' whispers Mimi, instinctively raising her head

41

and meeting the eyes of a middle-aged man who is smiling in genuine admiration of Mimi's coiled red hair. Politely, Mimi smiles back. 'For God's sake,' hisses Betty. 'Don't encourage him. I shan't be able to get rid of him.' But she moves her chair slightly and, in the course of doing so, her skirt rides up a little. She appears not to notice this. The middle-aged man, however, recognizes the difference between the two sisters and adjusts his manner accordingly, turning his attention to Betty, albeit with some slight feeling of regret. Most people are aware that Betty is inferior to her sister but Betty provokes and absorbs so much attention that she is usually thought of as more interesting, more controversial, more entertaining. Betty has a trace of Frederick's command of alluring bad behaviour. In any contest with her sister, one, to be sure, which Betty might care to avoid, there is no doubt as to which one will carry the day.

That is why there is something of a question mark over the sisters' relations with Frank Cariani. Handsome Frank, although all too willing to make an exhibition of himself when he dances with Betty, really prefers the docile and serious Mimi, whose grave demeanour appeals to his rigorous Italian upbringing. It is Mimi whom he slips round the door of the music room to see although his visits are cut short by Betty whirling him off for a bout of passionate Latin dancing. Betty is one of those women who believe in acting out a passion before they really feel it. Maybe they are cold. Maybe Betty, for all her exacerbated appetites, suspects this of herself. Maybe she knows that Mimi, so dreamy, so passive, so correct, might, would, with the right partner, come to a deep amorous understanding, an expansive love without need of gestures, a radiant acceptance of what a man has to offer, and a joyous capacity for motherhood that Betty knows can never be hers. Perhaps that is why she starts to try harder to attract Frank Cariani's attention, pressing up against his body in long silent attitudes not wholly warranted by the dance, or, dropping all pretence, touching him knowingly, her sharp little tongue just visible between her sharp little teeth. Betty is not entirely bad. She wants to capture Frank Cariani before her sister comes to realize how much she cares about him. In that way, thinks Betty, Mimi will be spared what she might have felt had she, Betty, taken her time, as she would have preferred to do. It is imperative for a woman of Betty's temperament (and high spirits) not to cede the pass to any other woman even if that other woman should happen to be her sister. Knowing so much more about men, she has found herself obliged, by a single long and entirely serious glance between Mimi and Frank, to force the issue. Regrettable, but necessary.

That is why Betty has been obliged to make certain contingency plans when her removal to a finishing school in Switzerland is under active discussion. Betty knows that without her supervision Mimi might permit herself to become seriously enamoured of Frank Cariani and he of her. Mimi is one of those women who marry early or not at all, and she is, at this moment, very beautiful. Frank Cariani, although not of an eminence to please Sofka, would make an excellent son-in-law, attentive, deferential, respectful. The Cariani academy is doing so well that Mr Cariani senior has been able to buy the freehold of the house next door, extending himself quite patriarchally along Marylebone Lane. Mr Cariani senior is more than good to his wife, his unmarried sister, and his mother, and has housed a widowed sister-in-law in another property he happens to own somewhat to the north of Regent's Park. This is entirely the kind of benevolent and structured family into which Mimi might transfer from her mother's house without any feeling of disloyalty whatever, and Sofka, seeing her safe at last, could not but approve. In addition to all this, Frank Cariani is a very handsome man. For Betty, the idea that Mimi might see him naked before she herself does is simply not to be borne.

Betty's plan is to acquiesce to the finishing school idea, to suggest that Frederick accompany her as far as Paris, and that he then put her on the train to Lausanne. Knowing Frederick and his habits, she will be able to dissuade him from seeing her to the Gare de Lyon, since she has behaved so beautifully during their brief stay at the Hôtel Bedford et West End, not screaming, not demanding to drink champagne, not wearing outrageous clothes. Having said goodbye to Frederick, Betty will lie low for a couple of days until she knows him to have left Paris. She will then – and this is the difficult part – wait for Frank Cariani to join her. She has the better part of nine hundred pounds, she is quite fearless, she believes in their future as the highest-paid character dancers in Paris, and Frank is a simple fellow who is very tired of living under his father's thumb. He tells himself that once he has established himself as a reputable name in the entertainment world he can always go home and find Mimi again. Mimi is not the type of girl who will, or indeed, can, do anything independently. But Betty knows that her mission in life is to be a woman who prevents men from staying with their virgin loves, and she is eager to embark on this career.

On the day of Betty's departure for her school in Clarins, Sofka weeps as if she is saying goodbye to her for ever. Betty weeps too. There is a kind of random sorrow in Betty that guides her roughly to the inner meaning of these occasions. While the chauffeur loads the suitcases into the car, Betty embraces her mother and her sister. Only Alfred refuses to relax in her arms and turns his cheek stiffly for her kiss. Then the car moves off, very slowly, with a handkerchief fluttering at the window. On the street, Sofka, her own handkerchief quite soaked, suddenly grips Mimi by the hand, draws her to her side, and drops her head for a moment on to Mimi's shoulder. Mimi, surprised, smooths her mother's cheek. Sofka alone knows that she has sacrificed one daughter in order to keep the other.

F O U R

'DEAR NETTIE,' writes Alfred, aged sixteen. 'I hope you are well and happy. Thank you for your post-card showing the lake at sunset. It looks very pretty.'

Alfred sucks his pen and stares out of the window. He is not good at writing letters, perhaps because he is already very good at hiding his feelings. This he needs to do because he imagines his emotions to be so violent that they constitute a danger to others. His feelings are basically a love for Sofka and Mimi, a growing dislike of Frederick whom he sees as idle and flippant, decamping from his office in order, so he says, to give Alfred a taste of being in charge (at sixteen!), and sheer unbridled hatred of Betty, a response that surprises him, and which is in itself rather interesting. Alfred's purity reacts instinctively to another's impurity; what he feels for Betty is not in fact hatred but disgust. Alfred senses about Betty, when she passes him, a sharpish odour, the acid sweat of a true redhead, which makes him grit his teeth. In this way, and for this reason, he will always be resistant to the odours of women, shocking them sometimes by a very slight movement of recoil when they bend to kiss him. For this reason too he will only be accessible to a woman whom he recognizes as akin to himself, or to a woman so artificially fragrant that he does not sense her real presence.

Alfred's heavy burden of feeling, his purity, and his scorn have added a lowering quality to his handsome face which makes him doubly attractive to certain types of women, usually older women. He is perhaps Hippolytus to their Phaedra, and they look at his tall slim body, his long eyelashes, and the compressed line of his red lips and wonder how it would be to initiate him into the mysteries of love . . . Alfred, stern and unbendingly dutiful, inspires these feelings in a whole range of women, from Frederick's motherly secretary to one or two of Sofka's friends. All are careful to censor their reactions, allowing themselves only an anxious smiling concern for his condition. Alfred is preoccupied by his condition and therefore does not notice the range of female sensibilities to which he has access. When he is a little older, this imperviousness will drive women to unwise acts and statements, which they will later regret.

It is in any event the peach-like face and the silky hair of Nettie which form Alfred's unique wish for the company of a woman other than his mother or his elder sister. But he thinks of Nettie not as a woman, although at nearly sixteen she is all the woman she will ever be, but as a child, that beautiful over-excited over-tired child with eyes black as black glass, her head thrown back, her arms extended, as he tried to dance with her at that long-ago wedding and at two weddings since then. She always seemed to be straining after life in a way that troubled him, for he could imagine nothing better than to stay as he had been, as they had been. With his mother there to care for him and with Nettie to love, Alfred's dream is crystallized, and in a curious way this dream will survive unmodified throughout his adult life. It seems to Alfred that there are two kinds of love: the one that cares for your welfare, your food, your comfort, and the one that engages your wildest dreams and impulses. At this blessed point in his life, still in childhood, Alfred possesses both types of love, sacred and profane. He will grieve for such plenitude for ever after.

To Alfred Sofka is quite simply a deity, one who bends her cool lips to his hot cheek or smooths the hair from his forehead when she thinks he has been reading too much. She is the one whose disapproval he would do anything to avoid and whose pain he would burn to avenge. He knows no one as beautiful as Sofka, with a beauty that does not disturb, a beauty always smiling, never challenging, implying caresses of the kind that lull a child to sleep. Even his beloved sister Mimi would do better, thinks Alfred, to follow Sofka in this respect, for Mimi, although good as gold, is also young and he senses in her an innocent stirring which to him spells corruption. It is the love that knows no questing and no conclusion that appeals to Alfred, and he does not yet know that he will not find it on this earth, for he thinks that he has round it in Sofka. And Sofka treats him like the man he has been forced to become. As he departs for the factory every morning, Sofka, in her Japanese silk *peignoir*, stands at the door to embrace him; she smooths his forehead once more, and hands him his newspaper, sending him off to the Westminster Bridge Road with his head held high, able to forget for a moment the grim day that lies ahead, in his pride at joining the community of the world's workers, in the knowledge that a loving and admiring woman will be waiting for him when he returns. In this way he experiences that good conscience that others never find, perhaps never look for. And when the door closes behind him, he knows that his mother will devote her morning to the grave and seemly pursuits of good house-keeping, and when he returns in the evening, tired with the unnatural tiredness of a young man grappling with an antipathy which he cannot overcome, he knows that

48

Sofka will have prepared for him the minced veal cutlet and the soft fruit pudding called *Kissel* that he prefers. He does not yet know that his antipathy is the price of his good conscience, and that in later life, bewildered by his inability to find further happiness, he will be reaping the reward of that antipathy and that good conscience, for having overcome that early hurdle he finds himself suspicious of those who take life more easily, and having wrestled the enemy of his boyhood to the ground and worsted it he does not know how to transact with those who have had a more fortunate passage. Some men are children all their lives because they have had admiring mothers who chronicle their every game of football and their every lovable misdemeanour. Alfred too has a mother who watches him, jealous lest a fact of his life escape her. But she has seen to it that his life never will escape her, for he is now locked into a family enterprise from which there is no honourable issue, no issue of choice, that is, but only violent disappearances, as Betty will find out. Sofka, instinctively, through love, but also through fear, has transferred her vigilance from Frederick to Alfred, like a prudent investor transferring funds from one bank to another. Frederick's light-heartedness, though so enjoyable, really does not measure up to Alfred's severity. Frederick is for leisure, for diversion, for entertainment; Alfred is for work, for investment, for security.

When Alfred leaves for the factory every morning, breathing conscientiously the only fresh air he will encounter until the evening, and breathing rather hard, as if his antipathy were already at work, he is unaware of the random enquiring glances sent in his direction by many girls and some women. He is aware only of the task before him, planning to plunge directly into the morning's work so that, in the hour he takes for lunch, he can pay a visit to Charing Cross Road where Mr Levy has put by an interesting six-volume edition of Shakespeare's plays, illustrated with photographs of contemporary actors and actresses in appropriate costume. Alfred cannot afford it but Mr Levy is touched by his attention to the books and is allowing him to pay a little towards them every week. For Alfred, although doing a man's work, is still drawing a boy's salary. This is thought to be good for him, for, unknown to himself, Alfred has been entered on a long course of character training by those who know better than he does. In this way his character will be trained – by privation, of course – beyond those of any whose friendship he is likely to seek. His character, in fact, will be a burden to him rather than an asset. But that is the way with good characters.

Alfred, trying to deal with the antipathy that this way of life has forced upon him, and trying also to deal with the good conscience which is perhaps only blamelessness in disguise and can be forfeited at any moment, knows from his reading that virtue is its own reward. This seems to him rather hard, for by the same token vice is also its own reward. But if he translates his predicament into fiction, if he views it as a pilgrimage or a perilous enterprise or an adventure, if, in fact, he thinks of himself as Henry V or as Nicholas Nickleby, then he can soldier on, comforted by the thought that his efforts and his determination and all his good behaviour will be crowned with success, recognition, apotheosis. In this way it even crosses his mind that when Nettie comes home she will find him admirable. He desires to be found admirable by Nettie, thinking himself entitled to this desire, since he has obeyed the rules so far. He has, above all, obeyed his mother in everything. He does not yet know that men who obey their mothers in everything rarely win the admiration of other women.

Alfred is a worthy character, although he has had worthiness thrust upon him. His only reward is the approbation of others: of Sofka, of Mimi, who admires him and almost understands him, of Frederick, who is so delighted that his sibling promises to relieve him of all responsibility that he laughingly defers to him on many matters and readily acknowledges that Alfred's judgment in business is already superior to his own. And there is Lautner who truly respects him. Without Lautner, of course, Alfred's apprenticeship would be infinitely harder than it is at present; without Lautner at his elbow, always prepared to make suggestions and to work late, Alfred would be much more restricted. And for two years, perhaps three, Alfred repays Lautner's care and thoroughness; by the age of twenty-one Alfred will know every detail of the workshops and the sheds and the warehouses and will be gravely cognisant of the people who labour for him. In the meantime, he refuses to take more than an hour for lunch and he works so regularly himself that there are fewer opportunities for Lautner to visit the house on Sunday evenings, for coffee and for marzipan cake. And as Lautner sees Alfred succeeding beyond his expectations, he is almost disappointed at his own growing distance from the family. Therefore he makes it his business sometimes to go over to the house with a message or a reminder or even a suggestion. 'You need not have bothered,' says Alfred who dislikes the incursion of his everyday life into those blessed truces which are observed at the weekends. 'It could have waited until tomorrow.'

It is therefore a terrible shock to Alfred's very hard-won equilibrium to get home one evening and to find Sofka in a state of considerable agitation over Betty. This is doubly unsettling to Alfred; he has never seen Sofka in a comparable state over himself, and in any event he judges Betty to be unworthy of his mother's care. As far as Alfred is concerned Betty is a futile and self-regarding girl and he begrudges her the money she has received on her eighteenth birthday. It now appears that, not content with her idleness and her money and her music lessons, Betty is to be allowed a long holiday in Switzerland at the family's expense. Worst of all, Betty will have access to Nettie for she is to be sent to the same establishment at Clarins where mysterious things are done to make girls worldly, educated, and poised. Like many another man, Alfred views this process with concern. If anyone is to go to Switzerland, let it be his sister Mimi whose vagueness could do with a little tempering; even Alfred can see that. But Mimi is of all things his friend; Mimi, knowing of the six-volume edition of Shakespeare coveted by Alfred, presented it to him the moment her money came through to her. In this way Alfred has received the ideal gift; he could not have bought it himself because he has only his salary, and part of that goes into the household expenses. Their father, in his wisdom, decreed that the girls should have money and the boys shares in the business. So Alfred, burdened with adult cares, is more than a little shocked that Betty should benefit from so much of their mother's concern.

However, he will be very glad to see the back of her. And of Frederick too, if the truth were known. He feels instinctively that Betty and Frederick form a natural pair, and that he and Mimi form another, quite different, alliance. Together and apart, Mimi and Alfred stand for those stolid and perhaps little regarded virtues of loyalty and fidelity and a scrupulous attention paid to the word or promise given or received. The house seems to him a friendlier place the moment Frederick and Betty are out of it, although he is a little hurt to see the extent of his mother's grief, when only Mimi and himself are left. For the three days of their absence Alfred is happier than he has been for some time; when he returns in the evening, it is to find a subdued and rather quiet Sofka, and to hear the strains of a Chopin *étude* drifting down from the old nursery without the interruption of Betty's high voice or the slight moral exasperation afforded to him by Frederick's ever good-humoured presence. And although Sofka looks preoccupied and somewhat sad, and although Mimi's presence does little to cheer her up, Alfred finds that his mother clings to him in a way that makes him feel very strong, as if he is in a better position to care for her alone than with all the others put together. He finds this heartening, and something of a sop to his injured pride.

His position as head of the household elect, to which he has been steadily moving and for which Sofka has been preparing him, is absolutely consolidated when Frederick returns. Frederick, who is under the impression that he has delivered Betty to the Lausanne train, is ready to receive congratulations, and indeed Sofka has prepared a congratulatory meal for him. It is in the course of this meal, and under the closest questioning from Alfred, that Frederick reveals that he last saw Betty at the Hôtel Bedford et West End the night before she was due to leave for Lausanne and he to see her to the train. It was with a promise of good conduct from Betty that Frederick sailed off into the blue Parisian evening for a late stroll and a last brandy. It is, after all, much easier for him to catch the morning train to London, and Betty is not a child. She is quite capable of catching a train at her age. 'She is quite capable of catching a train at her age,' he says affably to his mother, not focusing on her dawning look of uneasiness. 'How do you know she caught it?' demands Alfred stonily. 'Why wouldn't she catch it?' asks Frederick, his eyebrows lifted. 'It's not as if she knows anyone in Paris.' For a moment they sit, digesting this sentence. Try as they may, they cannot dispute it. Betty knows no one in Paris. She has not been there since she was a very small child, with her mother and her nurse and her father, just before he died. She must have remembered it, in some mysterious way, as an agreeable alternative to home, as a place where life is a holiday.

With a stifled exclamation, Sofka gets up from the table, dropping her napkin, and is on the telephone, placing a call to Mme Renaudin in Clarins. There is no conversation during her absence, but Alfred fixes Frederick with his increasingly stony glance. At that moment he feels that he can discount and discard his brother; it is almost a moment of triumph. Mimi is pale and frightened; she is also guilty, for she thinks she knows something of what Betty has in mind. If Mimi knew for certain what she thinks she knows she would faint with the grief of that knowledge; therefore she puts it away from her. But she cannot recover her colour, even when she reflects that her mother must be more anxious, and it is only due to her abiding innocence that she does not in that moment renounce her obligations altogether.

In the brief interval of Sofka's absence, telephoning to Mme Renaudin, Frederick's status has undergone a slight but permanent alteration. Frederick's agreeable light-heartedness is perceived in that moment as unreliability, and when Sofka returns, pale and with a fixed expression, she ignores the hand he thrusts out towards her and waits for him to get to his feet and pull out her chair. 'She has not arrived,' Sofka finally says, after what seems a very long period of silence. Mimi puts her hands to her face. 'Alfred,' says Sofka, turning to him and disregarding the other two. 'You had better ring the hotel. If she is still there, I'm afraid you will have to go and get her back.'

It transpires that Betty has left the Hôtel Bedford et West End, that she in fact left when she was meant to, so as not to arouse undue suspicion. But she has not gone to Lausanne. She has moved to another, smaller hotel, the Hôtel des Acacias, the address of which she has deposited with the hall porter. How she got hold of this none of them can work out. It happens to be where Frank Cariani's family stay when they are in Paris, and it must have been Frank who mentioned this in the course of a long-ago conversation. But Mimi, who was also present when that conversation – a mere exchange of pleasantries – took place, at the very beginning of the girls' association with members of the Cariani family, is suddenly as cold as death. She imagines that it was Frank and Frank alone who planned this coup and for the first time in her life she recognizes the sad need to defend herself. 'If Alfred is going to Paris,' she says, 'I am going with him.' 'Good idea,' agrees Frederick. 'Paris is very charming at this time of the year. You are all making a fuss about nothing. I will stay here and keep Mama company.' None of them acknowledges this remark.

Stern but in full control, Alfred stands at the window the following morning, waiting for the car to come round. Mimi is a little delayed; as usual, before any sort of a journey, she feels unwell. She does, in fact, need all the forces at her command in order to accomplish this mission, although she does not quite know what she is going to do. One thing is certain: Betty is to be brought home. If nothing is said – and it would be better if nothing were said – then the implications of this desertion need not haunt her, and somehow they will all get over it. The unmentionable act, the image of which Mimi finds constantly in her mind, will have been, if not avoided, then certainly not consummated. That is all she can hope for now, and she begins to see, sadly, that this must be enough. She begins, in the way of all those who are born to lose, to imagine her way past this terrible damage and to try and regain favour in Frank Cariani's eyes. She will, she thinks, have a cheerful but honest explanation with him; no reproaches, of course, merely an indication of how she herself feels. Being a decent fellow, Frank will then compare the conduct of the two sisters in his mind and be won over by Mimi's honesty. Mimi thinks that this is how hearts are won, not believing for a moment that Betty's is the surer way. Behind this belief lies an unbearable vision of the world's duplicity that must not come to full realization.

On the train they say little to each other, although Alfred is considerate towards his sister. He knows that she will have a bad crossing. He himself is filled with a rising tide of distaste for this adventure, although he still derives a certain comfort from his displacement of Frederick. He is young enough to take pride in his manliness, and in the feeling of his grateful mother's arms about him as she embraced him for the last time. He does not ask himself why Betty has chosen to disappear. He attributes this escapade to her basic instability, and he realizes, with a coldness which could be unrelenting, that she has exchanged an innocent sojourn in the company of Nettie for this grubby escapade in an unfamiliar hotel in Paris. His distaste, which is tempered in England by the knowledge of Frederick's loss of favour (for Alfred has always been jealous of him), swells almost out of control by the time they are in France. Jolting down the corridor of the French train, in an effort to buy a cup of coffee for the woebegone Mimi, Alfred is accosted by a rough-looking individual with a tray round his neck, and is forced to purchase a bottle of some nameless cordial for a very high price. While he picks up his change and tries to work out the tip, the individual becomes restless. '*Alors, Monsieur*,' he upbraids Alfred. '*C'est pour aujourd'hui ou pour demain?*' There is a further muffled altercation as Alfred attempts to squeeze past him; he stumbles a little and the man with the tray is not displeased.

This tiny incident puts Alfred off balance and when he is once again seated next to Mimi and the overhead wires and cables of the track seem to rush together as if anxious to reach the journey's end, he surveys his sister's pale face and suffering expression and tells her rather sharply to tidy herself up. Alfred is in fact in an agony of discomfort, feeling himself to be disregarded and unknown; although his French is excellent it is the French of Victor Hugo and it has not been of much use to him so far. And there is the business of the hotels to be sorted out – he imagines that they will have to get on the trail as soon as they arrive – and he is very hungry and they have brought too much luggage. Seeing him momentarily disconcerted, Mimi rallies her forces, and like the excellent sister that she is lays a hand on his arm and says, 'First things first. We will go to the hotel, take a hot bath, have a meal sent up, and get a good night's sleep. We have done quite enough for one day. Tomorrow we can start again.'

In this way, impervious to the globe-shaped lights and the ineffable blue Parisian evening, they struggle into a taxi and are speeded towards the Hôtel Bedford et West End. 'We must telephone Mama,' says Mimi, who, in her tiredness, has let down her hair and loosened the collar of her dress. Glancing sharply at her, Alfred is surprised to see Mimi looking so old, and is immediately glad that he has ordered a suite instead of the two rooms that were offered. Money is no problem. Their father, in one of his mysterious but so adult arrangements, has left certain funds in the care of a lawyer acting for a deceased partner, and Alfred supposes that this lawyer must be contacted as soon as possible so that they are not to starve. A further telephone call is put through and Alfred is reassured to hear a polite voice speaking in strongly accented English, which to him at that moment means infinitely more than the French of Victor Hugo. Maître Blin will send a representative to the hotel in the morning and will meet Monsieur Dorn at the bank; a signature is all that is needed.

This conversation, together with some hot soup and a glass of wine, restores Alfred's equilibrium. He sits with Mimi in their stuffy little salon until it seems reasonable to send her to bed. He hates to see her looking so wan and defenceless and hopes that she will have repaired herself by the morning. Left alone, he puts through another call to Sofka, and this time manages to be less testy and more reassuring. Sofka, more impressed by his testiness than by his slightly mechanical reassurances, praises him for his aptitude; already she is reacting to his assumption of control, having persuaded herself that this will carry the day. Left alone, and with no one to talk to, almost too keyed up to go to bed, Alfred pulls aside the curtain and gazes down on the rushing traffic of the Rue de Rivoli. Faced with all that speed, he knows a moment of discouragement. Leaning his head against the cold glass, he remembers that it is his birthday. He is seventeen years old.

F I V E

WHEN MIMI awakes, after a profound sleep, she is
strangely calm, passionless, devoid of all the fears
that usually beset her. For a short while she lies in the
broad French bed, gazing at the milky rectangle of light
that is only faintly obscured by the yellowish tulle curtains, for she was too tired, on the previous evening, to
let the maid in to make all secure for the night. She reviews
the events that have brought the two of them to Paris; she
is well aware of Alfred's distaste for this adventure, of his
misery at having to deal with his father's lawyer – a
meeting for which he would have liked to be thoroughly
briefed and prepared – and his discomfort in this vast,
shabby and respectable hotel. Alfred has rarely been away
from home before, does not remember being a baby in
Paris and never thought that he would make his first
excursion into that wide world, of which he has read so
much, in so unseemly and so wretched a cause. Mimi is
aware of his disappointment; she is also aware that his
birthday was spent largely on a French train, and although
she knows that Sofka will have prepared a festive meal
for Alfred to celebrate his return, it will seem as if he
is only being congratulated for having carried out her
wishes, not for any merit of his own. Mimi is aware of
all this. She knows, too, that her sister is lost to them,
and for a moment she falters as she remembers how they

used to brush each other's hair, dreamily, in the old nursery. But after this moment of weakness, she recovers and rediscovers that strange blessed calm that descended on her when she awoke that morning.

She bathes and dresses quietly; then, writing a note for Alfred to tell him that she will be back in time for lunch and that he is not to worry, she slips out of the door and runs lightly down the red-carpeted staircase. It has somehow come to her, without much thought on her part, that Alfred will recover his equilibrium if he is left to walk about Paris on his own for a short while, and that she, in the meantime, will proceed to the Hôtel des Acacias, there to confront Betty. She knows quite well that this meeting will in effect change nothing and she is prepared to say goodbye to Betty, this very morning, if necessary. In fact, rather than bring about this purely formal exchange, which, she knows, Alfred would only spoil, Mimi would rather like to know how things stand between her sister and Frank Cariani. In fact, Mimi is quite adamant on this point; she requires this knowledge, not in any spirit of panic or despair, but in order to plan her future conduct. Mimi is not even surprised to find herself thinking in these terms, so becalmed is she by the strangeness, yet the dreamlike familiarity of the pearl-grey Parisian morning. So radical has been the shift in her consciousness during those hours of perfect sleep that she is not even surprised to have exchanged the past, by which she was previously bound, for the present, which now absorbs all her attention.

Quite without her habitual nervousness, Mimi sits down outside a café in the Place des Pyramides and orders a cup of coffee and a croissant. No one seems to think she should not be there and she is served quickly and efficiently. Then she puts a discreet hand to the embroidered collar of her blouse, another discreet hand to her heavy chignon of hair, gets up, and crosses the street into the Tuileries gardens. She does not know why she has done this, for the Hôtel des Acacias is in the opposite direction, somewhere near the Parc Monceau. But it is still early, very early, and Mimi desires to use her few free moments in order to bring home from this strange visit some memory of her own. It is so beautiful there in the gardens, the only other presence being that of the tiny whispering water jets turned on to sprinkle the flowers in the beds. These flowers – begonias? – glow redly but their fierce colour is muted by the surrounding greyness of the dusty paths, the heavy dew on the grass, and the thick autumn mist that will shortly rise to reveal a majestic late sun. Mimi drifts noiselessly under the chestnut trees, now heavy with the last of their green leaves; already the sap has left them and the brown and gold colours have begun their invasion. Like a child, Mimi stoops and picks up a chestnut, green, prickly, and hard, too young to split and reveal its glossy fruit. Down the paths, past gesturing statues, mute, stern, occasionally agonized, Mimi walks sedately, as if conscious of the statues' august and adult passions. She skirts the round pond, where she strolled as a child with her nurse, and sets her course for the Place de la Concorde. Mimi knows Paris well; she used to accompany her parents when they came over for the Salon d'Automne, and this was one of her daily promenades. But in the solitude of this early morning she is able to notice the bones of a landscape that was previously hidden to her by a press of people: here, for example, are the curving stone balustrades that form, as it were, the prelude to that great enclosure, now alive with traffic, with the obelisk in the centre and the arch at the far end and the policemen's whistles putting an end to her morning reverie.

Mimi sits on an iron chair and brushes the whitish dust

from her shoes. Then two hands go up to the chignon and anchor the tortoiseshell pins more securely. Curiously enough, although the noise and bustle have now reached daytime proportions, Mimi is still undisturbed. Her mind touches lightly on the problem before her; in her imagination she sees the Hôtel des Acacias, a small dark corner building overhung by heavy trees. She knows that she will find Betty there, and that she will no longer be responsible for Betty's actions. To Mimi, in one of her rare moments of wisdom, comes the knowledge that she is no longer responsible for a person whose actions are so hidden and so damaging. If anything, Mimi desires to see this new Betty simply in order to document herself on the circumstances in which Betty has chosen to live. She knows perfectly well that these will not be entirely respectable, and her one desire is to spare Alfred the sight of an unmade bed, perhaps a smear of make-up on a not entirely clean morning face, a suspicious concierge, an airless smell in the corridor . . . Brought up against this, Mimi knows, Alfred will lose his temper, lose his head. Far better that she, Mimi, should make a survey, uninfluenced, undisturbed; she will then know how much, or rather, how little, to tell her mother.

Mimi descends the steps and gets into a taxi. 'Rue des Acacias,' she says to the driver. '*Déposez-moi au coin de la rue, s'il vous plaît.*' Throughout the brief drive she gazes unseeingly through the window at the streets now hectic with traffic and confusion. Her massive feeling of control has not yet left her, and she is mildly surprised but in a blessedly detached sort of way. It seems to her that she has somehow come into her own, that she has left behind not only Betty, but Alfred, Sofka, and Frederick, the one whom facially she most closely resembles. If she is to see them again, she feels, it will be as a different person. She has no clear idea what she means by this.

The Hôtel des Acacias is indeed exactly as she imagined it. It occupies the sharp angled corner of two streets and is bounded by a blind stone wall over which heavy trees lift very dark heads. The only thing that Mimi has not imagined is the extreme cleanliness and propriety of the place. There is no sullen concierge but an eager little woman ready to answer her questions; she stands behind a tiny counter with a tiny stand of postcards on it and is only too pleased to respond to Mimi's queries. Yes, Mademoiselle Dorn is staying there and the little woman is very glad to know that someone has come to see her; the young lady is perhaps *too* young to be staying there alone. Will Madame be requiring a room? No, says Mimi, thoughtfully; that will not be necessary. If she could just see Mademoiselle Dorn now? But of course. If Madame would just walk around the corner she will un-doubtedly find the young lady eating her breakfast at the café.

Mimi walks out of the Hôtel des Acacias, knowing that she will never return there. It is quite respectable, she will tell Sofka, and perfectly clean, and the owner seems to be quite a genuine sort of woman. She will not tell her that the place has the depressing air common to all small family-run enterprises, that there is a muted noise coming from behind a glass door which leads presumably to the family's own quarters, that she has glimpsed a little girl playing hopscotch outside the entrance, and that there is a very faint smell of *Eau de Javel* in the foyer. And that one has to go out for all one's meals. She has no doubt that Betty has not noticed any of these things, being too intent on herself and the scandals she proposes to bring about. Nevertheless, as Mimi rounds the corner by the blind stone wall and comes alongside the Café-Bar des Acacias, she is quite relieved and even moved to see Betty sitting there, dipping her bread into her coffee like a native, and lapping it up with one of those sideways turns of the head that her sister knows so well.

Calmly, Mimi sits down at the table opposite her sister. Over the coffee-cup Betty's eyes widen like a cat's, but then they narrow, and the cup is replaced wordlessly in the saucer. For a moment, nothing is said. 'I'm not going home,' says Betty finally. 'No,' says Mimi, again quite calmly. 'I don't suppose you are. Have you got enough money?' She goes on, again with this extraordinary calm and freedom, to tell Betty to write to her mother; to tell her too, although she knows that Alfred will be furious about this, to get in touch with Maître Blin if she needs any assistance. She then examines her sister and sees that she looks marvellous. In spite of the fact that Betty has already bought herself an inexpensive-looking fur jacket, which she is wearing over one of her violently printed silk dresses, Mimi sees that the instinct that brought Betty to Paris was entirely correct. Far from looking sordid or decrepit, as if age and sin had already taken their toll, Betty has a coral bloom in her cheeks that has nothing at all to do with make-up but owes something perhaps to the many strands of coral necklace that she has wound round her startlingly white throat. The coral braceleted hand that still holds the handle of the coffee-cup has coral-coloured nails, and the grey eyes that look at her so sharply are rimmed with a subtle grey shadow that has replaced the earlier applications of kohl. All at once Mimi is conscious of the fact that she must look as timeless as the Lady of Shalott in comparison, and is instantly aware that she should do something about it. 'How will you live?' she asks Betty, mildly pursuing a need to take home an answer. 'Don't worry about me,' replies Betty proudly. 'I've got an audition at the Moulin Rouge this afternoon.' She has too. She has simply walked into the place and asked them to take her on, and the manager, not a bad sort of man, is so amused that she has been told to report back this very afternoon to go through her paces.

For a little while the two sisters sit, their faces turned not to each other but to the grey street, an empty regular unmemorable street, almost suburban in its small daytime preoccupations. Opposite them, on the other side, is a little grocery store, and two women with heavy shopping bags stand outside and talk. A postman lopes by and they both greet him. A woman with a dog on a leash emerges from a nearby building and waves to the two women chatting outside the store. Everybody seems very friendly and reliable. At the counter in the Café-Bar des Acacias stand a group of workmen, with curious hats, splashed with plaster or white paint, pushed to the back of their heads. There is very muted conversation. Betty snaps her fingers and orders more coffee, then looks enquiringly at Mimi: you too? Yes, nods Mimi. So the sisters sit peaceably and drink their coffee in the warm and still grey morning air.

Their brief communion is shattered by the sight and sound of Frank Cariani, who appears round the corner labouring under the weight of a heavy suitcase. He seems unsurprised to see the two of them, as he is so used to seeing them together, but merely grins cheerfully and puts his suitcase down with a sigh of relief. It is quite clear to Mimi that he has just arrived, and the enormous burden of what she has managed not to think about slips away from her, leaving her blissfully happy. Frank too is happy, thinking that he must have imagined the slightly disagreeable undertones of this adventure, which had always disturbed him. Here are the two girls, together as usual, just as they used to be, on holiday, apparently, and here he is, being agreeable to them, as he has always been. Whatever he thought his plans were, he is more than

65

happy to abandon them, and he no doubt thinks that he can go home again with only a little explaining to do, and no bad conscience. He is aware, of course, that Betty has immediately started sparkling and pouting at him, but he is rather used to women doing this, so he takes little notice of her. He has booked a room at the Hôtel des Acacias, but then he never expected to stay anywhere else and thinks nothing of it. Why not enjoy a few days' holiday himself? His father owes him that much, and he has surreptitiously cancelled his lessons for the coming week. In a moment he will send a telegram to his father, saying that he has accepted a last-minute invitation from a friend. This is, in a way, true. There will be mild trouble when he gets home, of course, but nothing that he can't deal with, as long as he has a clear conscience.

When the three of them have exchanged polite and friendly greetings and have sat together over yet another cup of coffee, Mimi, still fully in command, gets up and makes as if to leave. The other two look up at her, waiting for her to do something. 'Betty,' says Mimi. 'I will tell Mama to expect you home in a week's time. Don't forget to get in touch with Maître Blin. He will arrange about your ticket.' Betty looks furious but says nothing. She has no intention of going home, as they both know, but she feels that she has lost face by being instructed in this manner. 'Frank,' says Mimi calmly, as if she has been talking privately to him all her life. 'Will you walk me to a taxi? I think I saw a rank just round the corner.' Frank assents with alacrity, and is only momentarily intercepted by Betty who embraces him, head back, leg bent back at the knee, as if he were going on a long journey. The workmen in the café cheer her with good-natured amusement. Both sisters blush deeply at this. It is their last moment of common feeling.

As Frank strides beside her on his beautifully elastic

dancer's legs Mimi wonders how she is to move ahead.
For a moment, and quite unexpectedly, she is tired, sad,
faintly ashamed of this whole adventure. She knows
that she should have remained the correct elder sister,
negotiating Betty's return far more energetically than she
has done. How will life be for her without Betty? They
have never been apart before. She is aware that they have
both lost their early innocence, and she is aware of the
strangeness of this thought, for she has done nothing.
Betty has chosen to rid herself publicly and scandalously
of her girlhood, her upbringing, her education, even her
ancestry, but she, Mimi, has done nothing. Disturbed,
she turns to Frank. 'She must be home by next week,' she
says to him. 'She is foolish and headstrong and she worries
our mother.' 'Never fear,' says Frank. 'I will bring her
home.' At this Mimi looks at him with large sad eyes.
'Don't hurt her,' says Mimi with difficulty, not knowing
how to phrase this. 'Of course not,' he replies, without
difficulty, she thinks, in the painfully aware state that
seems to have succeeded her earlier calm. She puts out
her hand. 'Goodbye, Frank.' He retains her hand in his.
'I always liked you best, you know.' Her pain deepens,
then lightens, leaving her calm once again, but very sad.
'I am at the Hôtel Bedford et West End,' she tells him.
'And I shall be there all this evening.' He presses her hand
in acknowledgment before seeing her into the taxi.

Mimi finds Alfred looking brighter, after his visit to
the bank, and mildly pleased with his morning's work.
Apparently they have quite a lot of money, which is
always reassuring. 'Would you like to stay here a few
days?' asks Mimi, after she has explained that Betty will
return, under safe escort, in less than a week. 'No fear,'
says Alfred, who has not yet recovered from the un-
familiarity of this experience and who eyes approaching
waiters with deep suspicion. Decorously, they lunch in

their suite, for Alfred is in fact quite seriously disturbed by the French in their informal mode. He finds them threatening, confident, and much cleverer than he is, and he knows that at the bank they were expecting him to be Frederick. He is conscious of being young, although it was his birthday yesterday, and he is acutely homesick. The truth is that in some ways he has had to grow up too quickly and in others he has not had time to grow up at all. Alfred is a clever boy, and he is conscious of the fact that he is going to have to sort this out for himself. His heart is quite heavy at the prospect, and he pushes the creamed spinach to the side of his plate. Mimi, who has been watching him carefully, puts her hand on his. 'You can catch the three o'clock train,' she says. 'There's no point in our both being here. I'll stay until tomorrow. I'd like to buy one or two things.' Alfred's face brightens. 'Don't worry,' says Mimi. 'And tell them not to worry at home.' Yet even as she says this she knows that this Parisian escapade will not damage the people at home half so much as it will damage Alfred and herself.

After seeing Alfred off on the train and waving until both he and the train are out of sight, Mimi retraces her steps through the grimy arcades of the station and emerges once again into the full glory of the September afternoon. For a moment or two she is uncertain what to do, where to go, what to wait for, and how long to wait for it. But the powdery golden sun, made fragile and more beautiful by the knowledge, shared by all those people in the streets, that the year is dying, reassures her, and, without quite retrieving that passionless calm that was hers on waking, she is able to walk easily and devoid of forethought along the broad pavements and to admire the quick life around her, although she feels herself to be isolated in its midst.

Such physical solitude is quite unknown to her for she has always been happiest when protected by her family.

She alone remembers her father with affection and with nostalgia for his benevolent if abstracted presence. She was always secretly conscious of being his favourite and from the memory of his hand stroking her long red hair or producing chocolates for her from a silver box she has learnt to yearn for that aura of masculinity which intrigues a woman, tempts her, and makes her long to satisfy her curiosity. With Mimi, this is all below the surface, far below. She only knows that at home with Sofka and Frederick and Alfred and recently Betty she has been questing unconsciously for that man, that alien, that stranger, that appointed one, who will deliver her, the sleepwalker, from her sleep. Thus, in the bosom of her family, Mimi, the good daughter, has been the one most ready, most willing, to defect.

Here she is in Paris, on the first step of that defection, not knowing yet what it is but extraordinarily bold in answering its still extremely muted promptings. Here she is, about to embark on an adventure which is proportionately greater even than Betty's, yet she hardly sees what shape it will take, only that it has given her vague life an immediate direction. Isn't this enough? For women like Mimi it is enough. She does not know what to expect of the evening before her. She has made no firm appointment with Frank Cariani, but all the time she is drawing him towards her, invoking him, with the full force of her passive dreaming nature. Of Frank himself she knows nothing, only that he is the agent of this extraordinary change. Of Frank she merely perceives that he is beautiful and kind, a friend, a brother, yet definitely, astoundingly, desirably, other. She knows that he will be hers. Or rather, that she will be his.

In the Rue de Rivoli she stops instinctively outside a hairdresser's, then pushes open the door and goes in. She asks to have her hair cut, but when the hairdresser takes

69

the tortoiseshell pins out of her chignon he exclaims with admiration and refuses to touch it. Amorously he brushes the red-gold waves, turning them with his brush this way and that; smart women waiting for his attentions join in the chorus of admiration and suddenly Mimi is suffused with happiness. She sits, glowing, her hair spread over her shoulders; she closes her eyes and takes a deep breath. She looks like Rossetti's 'Beata Beatrix' which she has seen in a reproduction in Alfred's collection. After this moment of happiness she submits to having her hair washed and dried and her chignon put up again. The hairdresser and his clients smile kindly at her as she makes her faltering yet curiously stately exit.

The sun has lost its heat and is beginning to veil itself once more in greyish mist. As she sits drinking a cup of tea in that same café in the Place des Pyramides where she drank her coffee very early that morning Mimi feels coldness in the air, and the brief majesty of the hour, in which sights and sounds and smells are now so great as to seem impersonal, impels her to think ahead. She imagines that Frank will come to the hotel at about six o'clock; she finds this idea preformed in her mind and nothing will shift it. She knows, for example, that she has not missed him, that he is yet to come. She will have time for a bath before then and she will sit in her little salon and wait for him.

Dressed in her best cream silk dress, she sits by the window and watches the moon rise above the Tuileries. It has now turned seven and she is beginning to feel hungry. She calculates that in half an hour she will ask for a sandwich and some coffee to be brought up, so that when Frank comes – and he will now probably want to take her out to dinner – she will not have spoiled her appetite. By this time she is so awake, so ardent, that all appetites seem inexhaustible. At eight o'clock she asks for her sandwich and eats it absent-mindedly, still bound up in this extraordinary dream of love that fulfils her imaginatively over and above the circumstances of the time, the place, and the hour. At nine o'clock she leans back in her chair, a little tired, her eyes still wide with the vision of Frank's arrival. She is aware that at some point a maid has turned down the bed and has left the room silently with the tray. A little later it comes to her with the force of a revelation that Frank has had to dine with Betty, that he will see her back to the Hôtel des Acacias, and will then make his way across the city to the Rue de Rivoli: Mimi's impression that Frank will call to take her out to dinner is suddenly overtaken by the much stronger impression that he will now steal into her room like a lover, like a thief in the night. Hastily she removes her dress and pulls down her hair; then, in her plain white nightgown, she resumes her seat by the window. Since she can now see nothing she listens all the more intently. She hears the occasional motor car; she hears footsteps in the corridor and the diminishing sound of voices. She seems to hear a clangorous bell, although there are no churches in this district and the bell is probably in her head. The intense darkness envelops her, envelops also her inviolate dream. At some time in that interminable night she lies down on her bed; on her face the smile is tinged with intimations of the most absolute horror.

In the morning Mimi leaves Paris, a city to which she will never return.

S I X

WHO IS THIS person whom Frederick has brought home for coffee and for marzipan cake? She is certainly not a lady and is rather too old to be a girl: Sofka is almost forced to think of her as a woman. Where did he find her? At what party, in what clubhouse, on what golf-course or tennis-court did he manage to acquire this all-round, outdoor, noisy, cheery, healthy-looking, loud-voiced, incessantly laughing, large-boned, carelessly dressed person whose name is Eva and who instantly says, 'Call me Evie'? Why should Sofka call her Evie, even if the woman has unconsciously conformed to Sofka's family tradition? Why should she call her anything, thinks Sofka, as Evie, legs spread comfortably apart, gleaming teeth well in evidence, skirt slightly twisted, holds out a large hand for another cup of coffee and appears to think it quite appropriate that she should be entertained in this manner? Sofka is full of immediate thoughts of rage as she cuts a final slice of marzipan cake and watches Frederick proffer it to his friend. 'Dolly telephoned,' she informs Frederick in a voice that is slightly higher than usual. 'She wants you to take her to a party. My son is in great demand,' she informs Evie with a smile of forbearance. 'I know,' laughs Evie, with another showing of what seem to Sofka to be giant-sized teeth. 'He's in great demand with me too.' At this Frederick laughs in a subservient manner that, to Sofka, is both fatuous and dangerous. A cold hand clutches at Sofka's heart. Where once she thought she feared for her daughters, she can now no longer deny herself the knowledge that it is her sons who are more precious to her. She prepares to fight for Frederick's virtue and for his continuance.

First, she must study her adversary, who should be easy to outwit. Evie gives the impression that she is of a slightly lower order of accomplishment than the girls who usually besiege Frederick. She seems, moreover, to be extraordinarily noisy and to have the ability to displace any object in her vicinity. She conveys an idea of power which has nothing to do with charm. (Sofka believes that charm is indispensable.) In addition to this idea of power, which is in effect little more than restlessness, but none the less menacing for that, Evie gives an impression, greatly exaggerated, of size. Sofka is somehow persuaded that Evie has huge primeval hands and thighs, the teeth of a shark, the braced back of a giant-killer. Evie is in fact of middle height and average weight; she has, to be sure, rather large hands, but she is not bad-looking. She is not bad-looking if you abandon all thoughts of feminine beauty in the more regular or conservative sense: Evie is not bad-looking as a member of the species. And it is as a member of the species, in those days before the lava cooled, that she is most viable. That is Evie's trump card: viability. With her strong neck, ready smile, woodcutter's teeth, and unvarnished good health, Evie seems to promise, on her own, the propagation of the race. Next to her, Frederick appears effete, decorative, luxurious; Frederick reverts to being a violin player, no longer with the panache of the orchestral conductor whom he once resembled but rather like the leader of a trio in some provincial coffee-house, a little bulky, still radiantly

good-tempered, but with some of his bloom gone for
ever. When she sees this, Sofka mourns inwardly as if
Frederick were already lost to her.

It is a long time since Frederick did a proper day's work.
His visits to the factory are now brief, and, to tell the
truth, they are not encouraged by Alfred, who, with
Lautner as his ally, is gradually assuming sole control.
Overseas buyers and representatives still ask after Frederick, rather missing his genial presence and his opulence
with the cigars and the coffee, but Alfred is becoming
adept at implying that Frederick is only a consultant these
days. In fact Frederick is not much of anything at all. He
attends perhaps two or three afternoons a week, still able
to cheer and inspire the secretaries and the typists, but not
altogether aware of what is going on. What he does
recognize is the growing power of Alfred's chilly personality. Alfred is the one person in the family whom he has
never been able to win over. In his easy-going way
Frederick is sorry for this; he quite liked Alfred as a little
boy, and he doesn't even mind him too much now.
Frederick bears no grudge against this slackening of the
fraternal bond; the bond was, perhaps, never much more
than an accident of birth, and in any event Frederick has
always been more fond of his mother and his sisters. It is
the astonishing fact that in spite of or perhaps because of
his great success with women, Frederick has a sort of
feminine sensibility. He adores women, he appreciates
them, he maddens them with his knowledge of their little
ploys. He bathes in an entirely feminine atmosphere, and
in this way subtly eludes that English persona that his
mother has decreed for him and reverts to more distant
origins. The violin player in the provincial coffee-house
was not altogether wide of the mark.

What then can he see in Evie? Evie is no oil painting,
and, as far as Sofka can discern, is entirely devoid of

feminine mystery. But this is where Sofka ignores the clues. Evie may not be feminine, but she is abundantly female. The spread thighs, the gleaming teeth, the shouting laughter, the springy yardage of hair: all these features speak a language which perhaps Sofka has never understood. But it is precisely this concentration of animality that has hooked Frederick and knocked him out. All those years of half-measures, of flattery and *badinage*, of conquests too easy because they were largely unsought, have dulled his appetite for dainty fare. He now seeks cataclysms and no longer cares for disguise.

Evie has yet another trump card, and that is power. Whereas Frederick is content to take the inert line that best suits his feminine personality, investing in life no more than his lazy good nature will tolerate, Evie has a will to succeed that might well terrify a lesser woman. Or indeed a lesser man. The traditional sort of woman in whose mould Sofka is irrevocably cast might rely on a mild and subtle influence compounded of glancing opinions, smiling obliquities, tender and persuasive flatteries, the occasional withdrawal into ancestral hauteur; these would be thought legitimate, permitted, respectable. But Evie, in her curiously blind fashion, wants certain things very much indeed and will exert a sort of menace until she gets them. This menace will be translated in a number of ways, largely physical: the restlessness will increase, the laughter become more incessant, the sort of teasing that verges on cruelty but which is covered by some semblance of rough good nature will be more in evidence, and in moments of real tension, shouting, crying, even fighting. All this is so much like Evie's particular form of love-making that Frederick is inevitably enslaved and usually does as Evie wants. Evie has only to throw back her head in a peal of laughter, revealing her trembling pink uvula, than Frederick is subjugated. Never before has he been so closely in touch with the mysteries of the flesh. For Frederick, despite all his winning ways, is a genuine voluptuary.

In her primitive manner, Evie squares up to Sofka, well aware of her fastidious opposition, although smiling pleasantries are still being exchanged. The marzipan cake is praised, the charming décor of Sofka's rosy damask drawing-room is appreciated; Sofka's opinion is sought on various unimportant issues. At the same time, Evie is laying down her cards. Her father is well off, very well off, in fact, and she is the only daughter. Her family is in the hotel business, and has been so for three generations; although Evie has been sent to England for her schooling, and although her papa has bought her a very attractive flat in Devonshire Place, her real home is on the Italian Riviera, where her papa owns several hotels on that blistering strip of coast between Nice and La Spezia. Clearly, Evie is her papa's girl, to judge from the number of times she mentions him. She has the sort of exotic bad manners, the complete conviction of her own uniqueness, that bespeak the adoration of a father rather than of a mother. To Sofka, so much her own mother's daughter, this is alien. She remembers her mother's whispering encouragement when she was on the verge of marriage, her mother's insistence on fine manners and fine linens and fine food . . . But this noisy girl is talking about shares and capital investments and foreign taxes and the advisability of acquiring property in several countries. It is quite clear, from the way this conversation is going, that Evie is the man in this arrangement and Frederick the woman. Evie is laying down favourable terms for taking Sofka's son off her hands. She has the money to do it and the power to make of Frederick what she will.

Evie, to Sofka's regret, becomes a regular Sunday

visitor. After a while, she is invited to lunch. This has been a rather mournful meal of late. Not only is Betty irrevocably missing, not only is Alfred – at the head of the table – stonily silent, but something has happened to Mimi, who is no longer the smiling and docile daughter that she used so beautifully to be. Picture them at the table. Alfred, flourishing carving knives, prepares to exert his patriarchal will on a large roast of beef, for Sunday is devoted to the consumption of traditional English food. This seems appropriate although Sofka finds it a little too robust for her appetite. Alfred sits at the head of the table because Sofka has decided that he deserves this distinction. She herself sits at the foot, and Frederick is on her right, where he prefers to be. These positions seem so appropriate to the natures of the two brothers that neither of them would think to dispute them, although Alfred has a lingering nostalgia for the days when Frederick sat at the head, and he, the cherished younger son, sat at Sofka's side, where, as a boy, he could turn to her and whisper requests. On Alfred's right hand sits Mimi, who seems to have lost a little weight or to have let her hair grow rather untidily; it is difficult to see at first glance what the alteration is, but Mimi seems to have forfeited that enchanting candour that she once possessed and with it that candour of appearance that so became her. She now looks older, a little gaunt at times; one is aware, as one never was before, that she is the sort of woman who loses her looks with her innocence. What has happened to Mimi no one knows; it is thought by Alfred that she caught a germ in France and is now in a state of convalescence which may take some time but which will inevitably lead to complete recovery. Sofka knows that something has happened, but will never permit herself to ask, lest her questions bruise the girl too much. She looks with pain at Mimi, who tends to fall these days into slight

77

absences, silences devoid of rancour, largely composed of dream. To Sofka, at these times, Mimi does indeed appear to be suffering from some sort of languor, and she defers to Alfred's verdict. Alfred remembers the nameless cordial that he purchased on the train; he remembers too the insults in which he was involved, and has no difficulty in associating this draught with Mimi's languor. The doctor has been consulted, and an iron tonic has been prescribed. This appears to have made no perceptible difference, but as Mimi presents no real evidence of illness, other than her increased mildness and quietness, the time has not yet come for stronger measures or for serious heart searchings. Her appetite is good, if a little mechanical.

On the other side of the table a chair has been removed, or rather set back against the wall. 'My younger daughter is in Paris,' explains Sofka. 'She is completing her education there.' Never did she speak a truer word. For some reason, some ancient sense of identification or approval, Sofka has decided to let Betty have her own way. Funds have been made available to her through the good offices of Maître Blin, who has also seen her installed in a respectable *pension* in the Avenue Mozart. There have been telephone calls to Betty every Friday evening, and when she comes away from the telephone Sofka allows a small smile to play round her lips. Does she secretly rejoice in this outrageous daughter who has the courage to break with the conventions? Does Sofka like the bad rather than the good in her children? If Mimi and Alfred are the alleged and established good son and daughter, deferred to and cherished for their very beautiful qualities, does Sofka nevertheless contemplate with a private delight Frederick's dissolute charm and Betty's nerveless insolence? 'Mama, Mama,' wheedles Betty on the telephone. 'Don't be cross with me, little Mama.' And she puts a kiss into the receiver which Sofka hears with a smile. As far as she knows, Betty, respectably housed, is taking singing and dancing lessons, which Sofka hopes she will forget about in due course. What Sofka does not know is that Frank Cariani is still there, albeit at the Hôtel des Acacias, and that under Betty's direction they have rehearsed a dance routine which the manager of the Moulin Rouge is going to let them try out mid-week when business is slack. They are billed as '*Bunny et Frank, danseurs de charme*'. Betty calls herself Bunny in Paris. She thinks it more chic.

Alfred flourishes his iron-age instruments and sets about carving the meat. This is the one meal of the week that Sofka does not supervise, leaving it to the housekeeper, who reproduces the Sunday dinners of her childhood: oozing beef, roast potatoes gleaming with fat, cabbage innocent of butter or of caraway seeds. With this, a sauceboat filled with gravy the colour of mulligatawny soup. Sofka finds this meal quite indigestible, but Alfred, for some reason, requests it and seems to enjoy it: Alfred has revealed a nostalgia for an English childhood known mainly through his reading for he never knew it in real life. Sofka's children have never been to school: they are outside every recognized norm. The boys had a tutor and the girls a governess. They wound up with numerous accomplishments but no real education; this is one of the reasons why they find it so difficult to mix with other young people. From childhood, their ways have been cast among their own kind, and their loyalties to their home and family reinforced by memories of unlimited reading in silent cigar-scented rooms, piano lessons, little recitals, and the chocolates produced from the silver box as a reward. Although this regime is bred into Alfred, he has learned from his reading of Charles Dickens that a more robust attitude pertains to hard labour and the eating of traditional food. Feeling himself to have laboured hard and long, albeit in a handsome office these days, Alfred asserts his honorary and Dickensian right to the roast beef of old England. He has shown himself a little impatient of the *douceurs* of Sofka's drawing-room of late, and has turned away from her spiced and subtle cooking. To his mind, Sofka's odourless yet rich jellied consommé cannot compare with the housekeeper's dense Scotch broth.

Evie enjoys this sort of food too. So overjoyed is she to be included in this ceremonial meal that she joins in as if she were already one of the family. Seizing a silver spoon she plunges it into the cabbage and hands on the loaded plates; Sofka's eyelids quiver as dishes are passed round and across the table in genial and plebeian fashion. But Evie is not abashed, and eats with hearty appetite, ready to refuel them all as she sits with spoon poised over the roast potatoes. She manages to talk as well as eat, and this is just as well because the others are on the whole silent. Truth to tell, Evie's heartiness is rather exhausting to witness and while none of them really approves of it they find it acceptable in the sense that it relieves them of all effort. Frederick is the only one who is listening to her. Sofka, eating minutely, studies her with grave and painful attention. Alfred, wondering, as always, why this food never tastes as good as he expected it to, doesn't mind Evie; he thinks she will do for Frederick as she is likely to take him over and keep him quiet. Only Mimi smiles gratefully at Evie. Instinctively, Mimi discerns in Evie a rough good nature that has something innocent about it. Innocence. Mimi finds herself still craving it, that perishable commodity, that pearl of reputation and of inward memory.

The meat is followed by a pie in a china dish that gushes forth steam as soon as its crust is cracked. This is accompanied by custard, and goes down very well with

Alfred and Evie. Then the plates are removed and into the centre of the long lace tablecloth are placed the two fretted purple and gold china dishes piled high with rather tasteless hothouse nectarines, the silver bonbonnières filled with almonds and muscatels, and the silver box of cigars. As Frederick and Alfred light their cigars their faces change, become hazy, ruminative, more adult, out of reach. This change to the ancestral mode lightens the atmosphere, and Sofka, with a sigh, looks round at her altered family. She acknowledges, after having fought against the idea, that Frederick will marry Evie, who may, indeed, prove to be a devoted daughter-in-law; she is, in truth, a good-hearted girl and marriage will almost certainly tone down that laugh and subdue her restlessness. Sofka is almost reconciled to the idea of Frederick living in Devonshire Place and being a consultant to his brother; if he observes these technicalities Sofka does not mind too much what he does with the rest of his time. And Evie has a sense of family, that much is clear from all her references to her papa whom she calls Dadda. Sofka knows that she can expect to see both Frederick and Evie every Sunday afternoon for coffee and cake.

But it appears that Evie is more devoted to her papa than was apparent at the first. Her one idea is to go back and live with him on the Riviera, taking Frederick with her. Being acutely female, Evie desires to separate Frederick from his mother, although in more moral ways she is prepared to be strictly loyal and respectful. But when Evie's papa, a short fat man with the high burnish of one who runs a successful private empire, pays a visit to Sofka – and it seems as if by this means the alliance is already cemented – it is clear that the price that Frederick will pay for the hand of his daughter is the general managership of the Hotel Windsor in Bordighera, a recent acquisition which Evie's father hopes in time to bring into line with his more prestigious establishments in San Remo and La Spezia. This is a blow to the heart to Sofka, although they all agree that it is a handsome offer and an ideal plan: Frederick is overjoyed. He loves the sun; he loves hotels; he loves company. He is tired of the factory and he longs to let Evie take care of his life. Before they have hammered out the final details it is all arranged.

There is another reason for Sofka to agree to this. Evie's papa has warned her privately of conditions in Europe and what they mean for families such as theirs. Wars, and rumours of war. Let the children scatter, let them put down roots, let them transplant. Sofka knows that they are safe enough for the time being. But she also knows that she can never go home again.

So here they are in the wedding photograph. It appears to be a very jolly occasion, but perhaps that impression is given by Evie who is laughing, her open mouth revealing her triumphant teeth. Evie is wearing white satin and is carrying lilies; she carries them as if they were some sporting accessory, a tennis racquet perhaps. The vee neck of her white satin dress reveals a longish triangle of skin, and the skirt, which flows into a train at the back, is carelessly hitched up to show her ankles, and her hefty feet buckled into white satin shoes with cuban heels and *diamanté* straps over the insteps. On her head is a sort of satin fender, worn a bare inch above the eyebrows. Where she has got this curiously old-fashioned outfit from Heaven alone knows; but as she refused all Sofka's advice and offers of help, it looks as if she has been guided by the saleslady at Whiteley's or Harrods and has come out of it rather badly. But she grins with unabashed cheerfulness, as does Frederick; together they present a double row of teeth and already they are beginning to show a marked resemblance. Linking arms, they turn to each other, mirroring each other's smile. They will be happy, no doubt of that. Less smiling, more thoughtful is the bridegroom's mother, in long grey lace, I am told, with a small hat largely composed of marabou feathers. The bridegroom's sister does not look well; she wears rose-pink velvet, and either it is too loose or perhaps she has lost more weight; in any event, it does not fit her and her face is sad. But the sensation of the photograph is Betty who has come over from Paris for the wedding; in apricot crêpe, if you please, with a little turban of the same material. Roguishly, she clasps her mama's arm and peers over her shoulder at the photographer. She knows that her presence at this wedding, and indeed her performance at it, are going to have to compensate for a lot of absence to follow.

The bride's parents seem quite amiable; fattish people, he looking fat in striped trousers, she looking fat in pale mauve chiffon, with a hat in sweet-pea colours: a terrible choice. They have the dark complexion of people with a year-round tan, and in the photograph they appear to have arrived from another continent. No one has Sofka's air of suffering majesty, but then the bridegroom's mother may be forgiven this expression, seeing that she will shortly say goodbye to her elder son. But the bride-groom's best man has made a very good impression on the visitors and the guests. Alfred, in tails, is as striking now as Frederick was at that earlier wedding. He is, of course, more handsome. Not only is he slimmer, straighter; he has a look of austerity about him, one might say nobility, that almost compensates for his brother's imminent departure. Strange how dispensable Frederick has suddenly become. Strange how the younger son has grown to resemble his mother. Those clear open eyes, that unflinching gravity of expression. For the girls at the wedding, waiting for the dancing to begin, it is no longer Frederick who is the prize; Frederick has been led off, like a trophy, by the one who showed the most muscle and who stayed the course the longest. But he is not much missed. It is Alfred now who is the more interesting proposition.

S E V E N

BETTY HAS taken so easily to her vagabond Parisian life
that one is tempted to think that there is some validity
in the theory of rootless cosmopolitanism which has been
applied to her and her kind. Every morning she trips out
of her one-room flat for milk and a roll and trips back
again to make her breakfast. This is the only meal she has
at home, for she cannot, of course, cook or housekeep,
and in any event she has a passion for cafés, bars, restaurants: she would spend her day in them if she could, and
frequently does. In the sharp air of that late November it
is Betty's delight to steal out in the early morning, buy
the warm bread, and then steal back to bed, also warm,
and lie there like a cat, dozing and stretching, until about
eleven o'clock. Then it is time for her bath, and the long
elaborate business of preparing herself for a day in the
public eye. Seated before her dressing-table, with its
light mist of peach-pink powder and the odd discarded
necklace, Betty makes up her flawless young face with
the expertise and the severity usually reserved for the
middle-aged. Unsparing are the glances she directs at
herself, noting a smudge in the lipstick or an uneven
shading on one cheek-bone. Does she see the bluish
shadows under the eyes which are a legacy of all her late
nights and dozing mornings? Probably not; in any event,
she looks marvellous.

The flat is a mess and Betty cannot always prevail on the concierge, Madame Mercier, to clean it. When she moved in, just before Frederick got married, it was because she was bored with the unyielding respectability of the Pension Mozart, and anyway it was too tiring to have to go round to the Hôtel des Acacias every night. She was lucky to find this place, for although it is small it is private and Frank can be here all the time when she wants him. Funnily enough, she quite likes being here on her own. It is not that Frank is not in love with her, but that he is too simply in love with her to satisfy Betty's tastes. Frank is one of those artless men who fall in love and take this condition to be a licence for reminiscence: childhood, schooldays, family stories – an endless stream of mildly affectionate talk and no surprises. This is not to Betty's taste at all. Betty surrounds herself with a drama and an excitement that leaves no time for anybody's childhood. Betty is so violently single-minded that she will flirt with herself if there is nobody else immediately available. Betty would like a man of moods and passions, apt to fly into jealous rages which neither of them need take seriously, with no childhood to speak of, slightly cruel and unreliable, knowing all the best places, theatrical, like herself, loving play rather than truth, faithful but pretending not to be, abusive and despairing: such a man she would understand perfectly. But for Frank, who turns up every morning in time to take Betty out to lunch and who will stay with her all day, being unable to think of anywhere else to go, and who will be with her all night if she wants him, and who will, in all this time, wear a sunny and slightly puzzled smile, and will long to tell her of some family holiday in the distant past or some anecdote about his married sister, but who is quite used to being ignored, Betty has little sympathy and less and less patience. For this reason she has taken to snapping at him quite viciously, usually in public; she likes to show off her power over him. So that Frank is not entirely happy; it has become apparent, even to him, that he is too respectable for her. She refuses to marry him, although he, like the honourable soul he is, has asked her. Marriage is not in Betty's plans at all, at least, not marriage to Frank. He is useful as an escort, and nothing more. Or rather, was useful. When Betty thinks of him she shrugs. And when Frank looks at her he becomes thoughtful. She has developed far beyond him, out of his reach. When she sends her laugh pealing through smoky restaurants late at night, and when people, or rather other men, turn round and watch her appreciatively, Frank begins to wonder what his mother and his sisters would have made of Betty had they known her. It is in any event inconceivable that they should meet her in her present state. Frank feels some moral discomfort at this dilemma, which was entirely of Betty's own making, although he does not allow himself to blame her. Not yet. He feels a genuine unhappiness at the irresolute and excitable nature of life here. Frank is really a man of solid upbringing and settled habits; apart from his startling gifts as a dancer he is as regular in his patterns of thought and behaviour as his father's metronome. He is conscientious and kind and, in Betty's view, hopelessly incorruptible. Perhaps he would have been happier with Mimi after all.

The discovery of this little apartment in the Rue Jouffroy was an event for Betty, and she decided firmly to begin her life again from this point. Like all self-renewing persons, she finds it easy to discard anything or anyone who has proved something of a disappointment. The Pension Mozart was very comfortable but it was stuffy and rather like the finishing school she so cleverly resisted attending. In the same way the money was useful and easy to come by but she was very tired of being lectured by Maître Blin who seemed to think she could live on far less than Betty herself thought she needed. What right had he to lecture her, she stormed at him, and then stormed out of the room, covering up in her mind the fact that he was on the point of refusing to pay any more of her bills. In that way she felt liberated from the Pension Mozart and all its respectability; if they wanted her to live like a Bohemian, then that is what she would do. A friend of hers, another dancer, as it happened, whose dressing-room she had briefly shared, was leaving to go on tour and offered Betty the rest of her lease. The dark little flat enchants Betty; it is warm and quiet, and yet if she opens the window wide and looks out she can see the softly lit interior of the *pâtisserie* opposite. This sight heartens her for some reason: she finds the idea of women eating cakes infinitely reassuring. Perhaps this vignette impresses her as being one of woman's true destiny, although she might have questioned this. Betty's plans for her own life are much more demanding. Perhaps she finds the sight of greed to be natural and consoling. Perhaps she finds some echo, some familial reminiscence, in the warm pink lights and the aroma of vanilla that sometimes wafts across to her. No matter. If she is ever lonely, and that is rarely, she has only to glance across the street, to see the ladies, in their fur coats, meeting each other for coffee and conversation. That is what her mother always liked to do. And although Betty never misses her family, she does occasionally think about her mother. Perhaps it is for that reason that she has instantly warmed to this respectable, bourgeois, and somewhat unexciting neigh-bourhood: she knows that her mother would have felt at home here. But this is all that she has retained of earlier influences.

The bourgeois residue, for example, does not stretch as far as to encompass any sort of housekeeping. Flimsy dresses are strewn over chairs, stockings trail in the basin, there is a half-eaten apple on the dressing-table, and the tissue paper in which the morning's croissant was wrapped has been screwed up and aimed unsuccessfully at the overflowing waste-paper basket. Really, thinks Betty, Madame Mercier is too bad. She was supposed to come yesterday, or was it the day before? In any case, she herself has no time to clear up because she is off to lunch with a producer at La Coupole, a place she adores. She also adores the idea of having lunch with a producer, although what he produces is not entirely clear. She wonders where he could have seen her dance, because she has not been dancing recently. After her fairly successful appearance with Frank at the Moulin Rouge, she did a few weeks' work there, but it was pretty hard going, and she knew in her heart of hearts that it was Frank who was the star. So she rather went off the idea of 'Bunny et Frank, danseurs de charme', and although Frank liked the regular work, having no Maître Blin to fall back on, Betty told him that he could carry on without her if that was what he wanted. Of course, that was not what he wanted: he simply could not conceive of dancing by himself. He is not enough of a narcissist to be a complete artist. And anyway he looked to Betty to make the decisions, as she had always done. Betty, in the meantime, is taking voice lessons. She has her eye on a film career now. And she thinks that this man at La Coupole might bear her in mind when an opportunity comes up. That is why she intends to make an impression.

The making of an impression involves her in an elaborate *toilette*, which leaves balls of pink cottonwool and empty screw-top jars all over the misty surface of the dressing-table. The finished product is attired in a cunning little violet wool dress with a peplum, shiny high-heeled shoes, and a great deal of Schiaparelli's *Shocking* dabbed behind her ears and on her wrists. Then, hastily covering up the unmade bed with the faded crimson cover, and kicking a pair of red sandals out of sight, Betty dons her inexpensive fur jacket and sails out into the Rue Jouffroy, ignoring the fact that Frank Cariani will shortly be knocking on her door as usual with an enquiring smile on his face, which has become increasingly diffident as Betty's dynamic and volatile temperament has become more emancipated. Like a healthy animal, Betty has a short attention in his solo spot at the Olympia Music Hall; there will quite literally not see him, not perceive him in space, let alone in her mind's eye. When he brings himself to her attention, she shrugs. As she has mentally discarded him, he no longer being useful to her plans, she wonders why he is still there. Betty's centrality is so great that she is able to ignore the fact that Frank is attracting some attention in his solo spot at the Olympia Music Hall; there is talk of his teaming up with a pretty young dancer so that they can improvise an apache routine (always popular). 'What do you think?' asks Frank with furrowed brow. Betty shrugs. 'Do what you like,' she says. 'But don't expect to see me again. Don't expect to remain on terms with me after a dirty trick like that.' And she reapplies rouge to her smouldering mouth and flirts quite openly with a man whom she can see over Frank's shoulder. After he raises a mild protest Betty is enabled to make a scene, which she greatly enjoys. Really, of the two of them, it is Betty who possesses the artistic temperament.

Being a healthy animal, Betty taps her way appreciatively down the Rue Jouffroy, inhaling the sharp cold clean air, and eyeing her reflection in the windows of shops. With this sense of well-being which comes to her unmediated by scrutiny and which is the greatest gift that nature could have bestowed on her, Betty is surrounded with an aura of confidence and expectation which assures the only sort of success that she values: acclaim. It was for acclaim that she began to dance, knowing that the applause greeting her final pose was not so much for the performance as for the provocation of her offered body. This is what she understands. And if she has stopped dancing, it is because she has realized that she can win the same sort of acclaim without going through the punishing routines of practising and rehearsal on which most managements seem to insist. When Betty remembers, she can twist her body into a charming little undulating walk, languorous but tongue-in-cheek, and can receive the same appreciation while walking down the street as she previously did when dancing the rumba, the tango, or the cachucha. She knows in her heart that such posturing is what Sofka would call *mauvais genre*, but she is above such considerations now. Or perhaps she is below them: as she is no longer supported by her family, needs must when the devil drives, and although she knows that all she has to do is to make reparation to Maître Blin and an act of contrition to the bank to have her funds restored, she has rather consigned those stratagems to the past, realizing, with that instinct that healthy animals possess, that where there is explaining to do she would rather leave no trace. For this reason her telephone calls home have become less frequent and are now rather stereotyped, relying on endearments which could, in time, become mechanical and are now beginning, just beginning, to appear so.

Anyway, she is meeting this man Markus for lunch, and rumour has it that he might be useful to her, as he spends half his time in America and that is where Betty would like to go. Although Paris is very beautiful and the adventure has been, on the whole, a success, Betty is ready to move on. And anyway, possessing the artistic temperament as she does, she feels she could bring a great deal of lustre and panache to the screen, and she starts to think of her appeal in wider, more brilliant terms. For those who seek acclaim are in love with the crowd, and, in time, only the plaudits of the crowd will satisfy them.

Betty has walked all the way to La Coupole, on her obedient, high-instepped dancer's feet, and the walk has brought out both her colour and that slightly sharp odour that excites some men and is about to have an immediate effect on Mr Markus. Mr Markus, Hungarian by origin, is a dark bulky man with troubled eyes, his heavy shoulders and arms decently shrouded by expensive suiting, his black and silver hair expertly barbered, a large gold ring on the little finger of his left hand which, even at this early hour, supports a massive cigar. Wearily but appreciatively, Mr Markus lumbers to his feet as Betty trips in, bows slightly, and kisses her hand. Despite his saturnine appearance, Mr Markus is a genuine film producer and he is almost entirely preoccupied with images rather-than realities. Nevertheless, his Hungarian eye notes Betty's immediate animal appeal and his senses register her range of appetite. In this, he is, of course, ahead of her, but Betty is willing to brazen it out until long experience will have made her a genuine expert. After Mr Markus has growled his usual rather extravagant greeting and after Betty has sparkled at him in return they both sit down and study the menu. As she is not paying, Betty orders caviare, steak, and *île flottante*.

With coffee, Betty relaxes, inserts a cigarette into a long holder, and leans back, surveying her favourite meeting place through eyes narrowed by smoke. La Coupole is full, as usual, and waiters force their way between the tables with trays held shoulder high; disappointed clients beg vainly for a seat. Betty sinks back against the velvet banquette with a sigh of pleasure. For a moment she has almost forgotten to make an impression on Mr Markus, who, unbeknownst to her, is watching her with genuine amusement. This child, he thinks, with her tiny fragment of experience, has the temperament of a great *allumeuse*: greedy, probably frigid, good-natured, vicious. Obviously well brought up but happier being less well brought up than her mother intended. Rich, well fed, well cared for: a glossy little girl but able to convey a marvellous impression of dirtiness. Mr Markus applies a match to his dead cigar and smiles, quite kindly. Well, if that is what she wants, he can give it to her. He will make her a bad girl on the screen – but only on the screen. While she half-closes her eyelids and moistens her lips for the benefit of an unseen audience, she will be remote from clutching hands, inviolate. Mr Markus, a man of great sophistication, knows that this will suit her very well for a time. When it no longer suits her, she will be of no further use to him.

Lifting a finger for the waiter, Mr Markus orders more coffee. 'I have to wait here until my nephew comes,' he explains to Betty. 'I asked him to meet me here. He is my assistant for the time being. My sister's son.' 'Oh, yes,' replies Betty, uninterested. Mr Markus frowns. He appreciates a show of good manners, even if the good manners are not there. He is a family man who likes to talk about families, but in this city, he finds, no one is interested in his family. Mr Markus sighs, with weariness and with homesickness. This troublesome nephew, whom he dislikes but who is the son of his beloved sister, has been wished on him; there is panic in Europe, a fact of which Betty is unaware, and a general desire to reach America. 'Take him,' Margit had pleaded. 'Take him with you.' And he had taken him. But the boy is insolent, quick-witted and hysterical, perhaps already unhinged by the separation from his home. Mr Markus, who loves his sister and who makes continental films with an English sound-track, takes the boy with a sigh. Every time he looks at him, he thinks of home.

When Betty first sets eyes on Max Markus she sees the cruel-eyed lover of her dreams. Max is a splendid feral creature with a narrow glossy head and dark plum-coloured eyes. He moves through the crowd contemptuously, a cigarette in his mouth, his jacket slung over one shoulder, his feet, in hand-made snakeskin shoes, carrying him effortlessly through the confusion and the press of people, a sheaf of papers in his hand. 'My nephew, Max,' says Mr Markus, with a helpless tremor of perception. 'Miss Dorn.' 'Bunny,' murmurs Betty, extending a hand. Max brings his heels together – a habit he is trying to forget – and bends low over the hand. Betty draws in a quivering breath. He pulls out a chair and sits astride it. 'Bunny?' he queries, with a wrinkling of his brow. 'What kind of a name is that? Is it your real name?' 'My stage name,' murmurs Betty, submissively. 'My real name is Babette.' 'Your stage name? What do you do?' Max Markus has this explosive and interrogatory habit of speech which makes everything he says sound provocative. Those who wish to rise to the bait may do so; others will have to learn to ignore it. Betty rises. 'I'm a dancer,' she says, bristling. Max Markus laughs. He also has a habit of laughing derisively after most remarks made by other people. Quite a lot of people find this offensive. To Betty it sounds deliciously masterful. It would be easy to have wonderful lovers' scenes with this extraordinary man, who is, she is sure, possessed of a volcanic temperament, and who is, in addition, Mr Markus's nephew. Half an hour after meeting Max Markus, who has taken his uncle's more influential surname, Betty does something entirely out of character. She falls in love with him.

With a sigh Mr Markus heaves himself to his feet,

leaving a handful of paper money beside the bill. 'You will excuse me,' he says to the preoccupied Betty. 'I must get back to my office. I will be in touch.' Then, turning to his nephew and attempting to read some kind of moral admonition into his glance, he suggests that Max should see Miss Dorn to the Place de la Concorde where she can catch a bus. Max accepts the suggestion but otherwise takes no notice. His way of asking Betty if he may accompany her is to remove his long legs from the chair, to sling his jacket over his shoulder once more, and, standing, to give a magnificent yawn, stretching his shoulders and his chest to great advantage. Obediently, Betty gets to her feet, then, recollecting herself, undulates past him, giving an answering display of waist and back muscles. Mr Markus, knowing that he is no longer relevant, lets Betty move ahead; he makes a sign to Max, and, as usual, slips him some money, which Max thrusts carelessly into his pocket.

Outside, they blink a little in the cold afternoon air. A weak whitish sun is making its last appearance of the season, and leaves fall silently from deserted trees. Max, coat over shoulder, strides ahead: Mr Markus places his Homburg hat over his heart, bows to Betty, and summons a taxi. Betty's mind is filled with confusion. She realizes that she will never be in control of a man like Max, and for once she does not care. But, not being in control, she does not know how to proceed, how to bridge the gap between walking along the Boulevard Saint-Germain with this stranger and enacting the fantasies which have been in her mind for as long as she can remember, now that she comes to think of it. For a while they walk in silence, Max always slightly ahead, Betty already slightly propitiatory in her attempts to catch up with him. After a few minutes she gives up the attempt and walks several paces behind him.

Max is in fact wretched and is covering up his wretchedness with bluster. He can only outwit circumstances by mocking them and by mocking everybody else. The more settled and secure they are, the more he interrogates them, laughing with incredulity at their polite replies. He desires a great deal yet it is not in him to ask for anything, so that when Betty suggests a cup of tea, he assents with a show of indifference which he does not feel. Naturally, Betty has chosen to desire a cup of tea outside Rumpelmayer's, which she vaguely remembers from Sofka's reminiscences, and once they are seated, under the pink shaded lamps, and they are both tackling the chestnut meringues which they find very much to their taste, she relaxes and retrieves her self-assurance. 'Are you in the film business too?' she asks, applying a violet georgette handkerchief delicately to the corners of her mouth. Max Markus utters a brutal and derisive laugh, designed to disconcert. 'Of course I am,' he replies. 'Did you think I was an accountant?' Actually he is a sort of office boy, but there is no doubt that he has capacities of some kind and the assurance that goes with accomplishment, whether it is real or only in the mind. It is homesickness that makes him coarse, and having to live up to his looks and be polite to his uncle, on whom he is dependent. In fact, fortunately for them both, Max Markus and his uncle see eye to eye in the making and framing of images, and when they walk along a street together, in this foreign Paris, and when the uncle points his cigar at an odd doorway or a cat creeping around a concierge's feet or a child carrying a long stick of bread the nephew assents eagerly, and, without words, describes with his hands, and a little advance or retreat, how it should be seen. They are in love, already nostalgically, with the life of the street, which they will transport to America. In this way, Max Markus finds himself studying Betty who, with fork poised, slowly turns a rosy pink under his gaze. Actually, what he sees is the outline of her hair against the lamp from the next table, and the deep indentations of her eyes, which he would light from beneath. Then he looks again, as Betty desires him to, and sees, with little surprise, that this young woman is in love with him and that he will be able to do with her what he wants.

What he wants, it appears, is roughly the same as what Betty wants: a full-fledged love affair lived entirely on the surface. In the darkening late afternoon he walks her back to her flat, he with his hands in his pockets, she with her hand through his arm. They stop at a bar for a drink and already they are launched on the pattern of their future behaviour: they are rather like that apache team that poor Frank is supposed to be thinking about. It takes them a very long time to get back to Betty's flat, and the words they have exchanged are entirely preoccupied, Betty with her thoughts, Max with his. In Betty's flat, their eyes brilliant with the progress of the evening, they finally turn to one another and take each other's measure. When they kiss, they are passionate, knowing. Max has been passionate and knowing since he was fifteen years old but Betty has not. Sitting on the edge of her bed, Max utters one last laugh, this time ruminative, reflective, before pulling Betty down beside him, and silencing any protests she might have been about to offer for the rest of the night.

E I G H T

O N THE EVE of the move to Bryanston Square, Sofka sits in her drawing-room for the last time, and with uncharacteristic nervousness, twists a handkerchief between her hands. It is not that she regrets leaving this house, although it has seen her happiest times; but the house has recently witnessed an unpleasant incident which makes it uncomfortable, as though it were a witness to a life of ease which is no longer appropriate. One afternoon, Sofka has been disturbed by a sound of voices at the front door, and then by the housekeeper asking her if she will come. Sofka, surprised, has gone to the door and has seen there, standing patiently on the step, a woman who seems vaguely familiar. This woman is dressed in decent black, a black coat which has been very expensive in its time, a rather stylish black straw hat, and a silk scarf, in excellent taste, open at the neck. All this bears the signs of stringent upkeep, perhaps beyond the bounds of its natural life. The woman's face is pale, expressionless, but composed; the pitiless blue eyes are direct. From a large tapestry bag at her feet, the woman produces some pieces of exquisite lace: collars, handkerchiefs, a shawl. 'Madam,' she says to Sofka. 'I have these things for sale. I have no money. You understand.' And with great dignity, and still with the pitiless gaze, she waits for Sofka's response.

'Irma,' says Sofka, after a long pause. 'Irma Beck. Is it you?'

At this the woman's face crumples, the eyes close, veiling the hideous gaze, and her body sways towards the open door, righting itself only as helping hands assist her and support her into the drawing-room. With a great effort, equal on both sides, Sofka and the woman sit with coffee-cups and discuss in measured terms what is to be done. Of the past, by common consent, they do not speak. It is too dangerous, too painful. Collapses might take place, youthful hopes might be remembered, wave after wave of reminiscence might be activated, and the woman gives Sofka to understand that nothing now must be cherished; only a dry appraisal of the possible is to be allowed. At last, and fearfully, Sofka enquires, 'Your children?' For the first time the woman relaxes, and smiles. 'Safe,' she says. 'Here.'

Rather than submit the woman to the indignity of receiving money, as if she were a beggar, Sofka arranges to visit her the following day, having carefully noted her address and calculating in her mind that she will use Lautner as an agent to transfer funds to this woman. In the meantime, they will continue to be two ladies who used, in the past, in another country, to know one another very slightly and who will keep up the acquaintance in as civilized a manner as can be guaranteed by the circumstances in which they find themselves.

As the woman, with bag intact, rises to leave, she extends her hand, and Sofka takes it. Then, wordlessly, the two women move into each other's arms and embrace, and wordlessly, composing themselves, they part.

Since that day Sofka has felt a tremor when she sits in her drawing-room or when she hears a step outside the front door. She has been able to ignore the two foreign girls in the kitchen, because they are young, and although given to outbursts of sobbing when certain pieces of music are being played, are also impudent and ruthless and beautiful, and will make their way in life. Indeed, in this house, they are more or less at home; under Sofka's guidance they are learning to be excellent *maîtresses de maison* and although they are not of an age to take pride in these things they will soon be very accomplished cooks. The housekeeper grumbles about them but she is near retiring age and is allowed to grumble anyway; she has been doing so for some time. When they move from the house to the flat in Bryanston Square, Sofka will take the opportunity to release her from service, with a handsome present that will enable her to go home to Somerset, as she has long wanted to do. She will take the two girls, Lili and Ursie (Ursula), with her to Bryanston Square. It will be a reduced household, and a rather different one. But the girls, Lili and Ursie, harsh hectic girls with unpredictable moods and extravagant loving impulses, have long fulfilled some emotional need of Sofka's; they serve in a sense to replace those children of hers who have gone, and they supplement, in some vital way, the excellent qualities of those children who remain.

It is, of course, the children who are gone whom Sofka mourns. Handsome Frederick and wicked Betty have taken all her heart with them, the one to Bordighera, the other to America. Of course, she is happy that they have married, although it seems to her terrible not to have been at Betty's hurried wedding in Paris, completed in a rush just before catching the boat. And to hear about it in a letter! It all happened so fast, pleaded Betty, and I am so happy. Promise you will come to America as soon as the war is over. Max sends love. Evie, in Bordighera, sends love too, and a request for various English commodities, not knowing these to be in short supply. Evie, as might have been expected, takes care of all the correspondence, leaving Frederick with no voice, maintaining him as an agreeable presence with no adult obligations other than to be charming and to amuse. In this way, Evie has proved to be the ideal wife for him. It is Evie, even when heavily pregnant, who is the guiding spirit behind the Hotel Windsor (soon to be cut off from all communication with home) and who busies herself with supplies and with staff and with matters of fuel and maintenance, while Frederick is usually to be found in the bar, a welcoming and hostly figure, to whom the ladies gravitate, their faces upturned like sunflowers when they hear his voice. He is particularly accomplished at the kind of flirtation which assumes deep inward intimacy but which never strays beyond the accepted formulae; his long years of practice have made him adept at this, and also untouched by it. He is, in many ways, completely happy.

It seems a little hard to Sofka that it is the most interesting of her children who have disappeared. She sees no connection between these two factors, although it is a connection often pondered, in deep secret, by Alfred. Unlike Frederick, Alfred has retained his looks, but the various discomforts which kept him aloof as a young man have intensified; he is now handsome, prosperous, and unforgiving. His years of unimpeded hard work have put a great deal of money into the bank but have brought no joy to him. With the disappearance of his brother and sister he feels the burden of unshared responsibility descend upon him; he is usually described as a devoted son. Certainly his gravity, his composure, would seem, to the uninformed observer, to suggest the acceptance of a way of life to which he has contributed so much. Even a certain testiness and a tendency to issue orders, at home as well as at the factory, bear witness to the cares and burdens of a man of affairs. Those affairs are, even now, secret and important, as the factory has been requisitioned, and Alfred with it. He is working for the government, and not even Sofka knows what he is doing. With the information that he would not be allowed to join the army but must do this essential and secret work at home, Alfred's last hope of escape disappeared. He was looking not so much for a means of serving his country as for an honourable discharge from family matters.

With a return of his old distaste, and with the irritability of his new imprisonment upon him, Alfred compensates by at last behaving like the rich man that he is. It is his idea to move back to Bryanston Square, having had some dim memory of living there as a small child, before the move to the house. He is the sort of man who composes himself by surveying his acres. The flat in Bryanston Square is greatly to his taste, although not to Sofka's, being almost entirely masculine in character. It was vacated in a hurry by a man in oil, seeking quieter pastures, and his handiwork is everywhere. Alfred feels particularly at home in the cigar-coloured drawing-room with the brown velvet curtains; after he has strewn his oriental rugs over the dense sheepskin carpet, and then, regretfully, taken them up again and removed them to his bedroom, Alfred feels there is little more to be done in the way of decoration. The oil man went in for strong dark colours; in addition to the brown drawing-room, there is a red dining-room, rather like the mouth of hell. Alfred masks the walls with his collection of framed political cartoons, which makes the room resemble the cloakroom of a gentleman's club. The common parts of the flat are dark green. All the bedrooms have a dull but expensive wallpaper, as if to signal that a lighter aspect of life might be enacted within their walls. The whole place is extravagantly warm and comfortable, if not exactly sympathetic. Behind the door to the kitchen quarters, Lili and Ursie can occasionally be heard shrieking with laughter. Whether they are laughing at the décor of the flat or at Alfred is very hard to tell. Sofka loves the sound of their irrepressible giggling so much that she never tries to discourage them.

Although the family has no intention of leaving London, despite its discomforts, Alfred almost immediately sets about looking for a house in the country. Perhaps he has been disappointed by the rapidity with which they have all come to terms with Bryanston Square. He has visions, largely nourished by reading, of the sort of home he has never known; this sort of home is bound up with a certain concept of the land, of rootedness, which is proving strangely elusive. In such a home, thinks Alfred, he will find his true centre; the aches and sorrows of childhood will disappear at last, never to return. For they have stayed with him, these sorrows. The effortfulness of being the model son has never quite disappeared, and the handsome face and the prosperous habits have never quite replaced the child in whose good character his mother took such a pride. Sometimes Alfred has a dream in which he is running through a dark wood; at his heels there are two beautiful golden dogs, his familiars, and with them he is running through the dark wood of his pilgrimage towards the golden dawn of his reward. It is this strange dream that has determined Alfred to look for his real home.

Dismissing from his mind the provocations of Lili, or possibly Ursie, Alfred once more sets out to try harder. If he finds this place it will be a sign that his efforts have been recognized; if he finds this place, thinks Alfred, he will put off the obedience of his youth and be his own man at last. Then, he promises himself, he will consume hecatombs of women, behave as badly as Frederick, care nothing for the feelings of others. He is like a man on a diet who has visions of outrageous excess, yet who is plagued by some inner and inalienable knowledge of checks and balances. If I do this, then I can do that. Why, one might object, why not do it anyway? But Alfred knows nothing of impulse, only of effort and hard work. And somewhere below the worldly manner and the increasing scepticism, there still burns the tiny but hardy flame of virtue which has sustained Alfred, much to his regret, for all of thirty years.

The excursions to the country take place in the car, now bereft of its chauffeur. Sofka remains at home, for she has become strangely quiet since the incident with Mrs Beck, and now sits for long afternoons in the cigar-coloured room, emerging only to tell the girls how to prepare the dinner and what sort of table to set. She does not believe in this country house of Alfred's, regarding it as irrelevant to their true needs. She sees these needs as unchanging and indeed unchangeable, although it appears that certain accommodations must be recognized. There is, for example, Mimi, who has long given rise to a certain vague disquiet. This disquiet has been overlaid, perhaps disguised, by her docile good manners, her charming devotion to her mother and her brother, her almost saintly self-effacement. Her health, too, has not been good, and has justified her stay-at-home existence. She still suffers from that strange languor that beset her on her return from Paris, and now has frequent headaches. Various bottles of pills have replaced the original iron tonic, but their only effect seems to be to make Mimi rather more tired. She still dresses beautifully and goes out, but she goes mostly to the hospital, where she does voluntary work of a vaguely conventual nature. All this reinforces the impression she gives of a maiden lady devoted to good works. Her beauty is still visible to those who never knew her earlier, but to Sofka's eyes it has undergone some tiny but irretrievable alteration. The high cheek-bones now accentuate the long slightly hollow cheeks and throw into relief the enormous eyes. And that marvellous hair, which she has never cut, seems to drag her down, massing its heavy coils on her neck like a bridle. She has never regained her lost fullness, and now appears hesitant, perhaps a little awkward, of no discernible age but of unvarying sweetness of expression. Fortunately there is no need for her to live any life other than the one she has decreed for herself. There is no need for Mimi to work, apart, of course, from the voluntary attendance at the hospital which she manages to expand until it fills most of her day. She gets home at about half-past four in the afternoon, to find Sofka waiting for her, with coffee. Sofka tries in vain to tempt her to eat; she has prepared little sandwiches for her. But Mimi is never hungry. After an hour with her mother Mimi goes into her bedroom which now houses the piano that used to be in the old nursery. Sometimes Sofka sits alone in the brown room and tries not to hear what Mimi is singing. 'O doux printemps d'autrefois . . .' sings Mimi, in her muted voice, and Sofka shivers. Then she makes her way to the kitchen, where the girls are involved in some passionate tearful argument, and Sofka resumes her old loving authority in her attempts to calm them down and to reconcile them.

Sofka feels for Mimi some of that old pain that she used to feel for her daughters when they were children. What will happen to them? Who will care for them? In the distraction of their growing up, and the turbulence of Betty's adolescence, this pain was almost forgotten. Now when Sofka looks at Mimi she feels not only the pain but a certain enmity, as if the good daughter had no right to disturb her later years with this unanswered question, this unsolved problem. It is clear now to Sofka that she is in a sense grateful to Frederick, to Betty, for recognizing that events must take their due and inevitable course, even if the means whereby they took that course were perhaps precipitate, inharmonious. What was once unwelcome is now thankfully acknowledged. But for Mimi she cannot lay down the burden and she casts about in her mind for some way of lightening it. The difficulty is that Mimi gives no cause for complaint apart from her unquestioning acceptance of her fate. Sofka now begins to feel that a little energy, a little heartlessness are called for. And she sees no way of supplying them. Certain changes can only come about from outside. And Mimi herself does not appear to be aware of this. She seems perfectly happy with her mother, and she is devoted to her brother. She is also fond of the girls, Lili and Ursie, who are much more afraid of her than they are of Sofka. There is something about Mimi that makes the girls eye her warily, and then turn to each other with unspoken comment. There is something there that they do not wish to see. This is the impression that Mimi gives to those who know her best.

Curiously enough, it is Alfred who desires Mimi's company. They set off together in the car to visit various properties, for Alfred is now more than ever intent on finding his mythical home, the one that will be his, the one that nobody can take away from him. He is a harsh and unforgiving driver, taking the corners sharply, always going too fast, muttering under his breath at the condition of the road or the stupidity of other motorists. All of this increases Mimi's discomfort, for she has never been a good passenger, sensing in the movement of the car a will much stronger than her own. These excursions always follow the same pattern, and they occur at regular intervals. Alfred drives furiously to some country town, where he has arranged to pick up the keys to various vacant properties. Mimi emerges shakily from the car and is set down outside a tea-shop, in which she repairs her nerves as best she can. In due course Alfred reappears, tight-lipped. 'No good?' enquires Mimi. 'No good,' he utters, as if it were the end of the world. This search, for him, has become a mythic quest, as it were for the grail. It sometimes seems to him that if the house were to appear, at the end of a long vista, intact, with smoke curling from its chimneys and the golden dogs on the lawn, he might be granted a moment of total recognition before expiring altogether. But for a long time the house refuses to appear, and as Alfred tramps back down the high street of whichever little town has seemed to him to be relevant he has the air of a veteran, dispossessed of all his belongings, returning from the wars.

Finally, and perhaps because the metaphorical implications of these wanderings have become too insistent to be borne, he buys a house, although why this house and not another they will never fully understand. Wren House is quite recklessly inconvenient, and despite its name, which refers not to the architect but to the bird, has the appearance of a large and curiously rebarbative cottage. As the car rocks up a hilly incline, the Kentish orchards on either side seem to groan with the weight of the apples bowing down their twisted branches. Apart from a garage which also houses a sub-post office, there is no other sign of human habitation. There are, however, three bungalows, almost hidden in a little defile, which seem to contain several small children. The parents of these children, Alfred explains proudly to Mimi, will perform various functions at Wren House. There will be someone to cut the logs and plant a very large vegetable garden, someone to clean, and a cook-housekeeper who will eventually occupy one of the small rooms at the top of the house. In fact, all the rooms are small, although there are rather a lot of them. Standing in any one of these rooms, it is possible to look straight into the side of a voluptuous but obtrusive green hill. Only at the back, in the kitchen, is there any sense of release from this geographical accident. The kitchen, soon to be taken over by the housekeeper, is a large pleasant room, and its back door opens on to a garden which becomes an orchard. Alfred reflects that all these apples will soon be his. Yet he still misses that sense of coming home, and he resolves to acquire two golden retrievers as soon as possible and to see if they make that essential difference.

In due course all weekends are spent at Wren House. Since none of the ancestral furniture will get through the door, let alone fit into the rooms, Alfred has bought some quite nice pieces at country auctions. He has found sofas, and tallboys, and a pretty oval dining-table. These he has had to supplement with beds from the Army and Navy Stores, and, in a gesture of independence, has purchased some massively oversprung divans which, with the addition of new eiderdowns and counterpanes, give the place the look of an hotel. Sofka says nothing. 'It is his life,' she explains to herself. She endures the divans and the kitchen garden and the children hanging over the gate; when she can force herself to overlook these things she sees that the countryside is very pretty, and that Mimi is looking much better in this good air. What she cannot quite get over or come to terms with is the housekeeper, Muriel. This distressing addition to the family, and indeed to the oval dining-table, where she dispenses meals, must be treated with smiling reserve, a reserve which Muriel does nothing to reciprocate. Muriel is a robust country-woman with the instincts of a back-street survivor. She is indulgent to the children of the neighbourhood who can often be found in the kitchen, and despite her preference for her own family and friends, many of whom have profited from Alfred's lavish housekeeping allowance, is kind enough to treat Sofka and Mimi as if they were old acquaintances of a faintly unfortunate nature. 'A little more for Mother?' she enquires, with a steaming ladle held aloft. Sofka, repressing a shudder, smilingly shakes her head. At last Alfred is able to enjoy those terrible meals he has read about and which he thinks he likes. Muriel is a lavish but uninteresting cook, made fearless by the amount of produce she is able to afford. Yet it is less her cooking that offends Sofka than her appearance, and particularly her appearance at table, where Sofka has no wish to see her. A satin blouse of dubious vintage and an even more dubious pair of trousers greet Sofka's uninflected gaze; there is a faint smell of Muriel's cat, whom Muriel greatly loves and to whom she addresses most of her remarks. 'Alfred,' says Sofka, after the first of such meals. 'That woman will have to go.' 'Nonsense, Mama,' says Alfred, more in the interests of territoriality than of wisdom. 'She fits in here very well. And she's a good sort, when you get to know her. You will just have to try to adapt.' They are both aghast at this remark, but Sofka, with remarkable stoicism, accepts it. 'Well, Alfred,' she replies, after a terrifying pause. 'It is your life.'

In view of this conversation, which Muriel has overheard, her independence increases. Soon it is quite common for Alfred to suggest, 'Mimi, give Muriel a hand, will you?' Since Muriel grumbles at the amount of work she has to do at the weekends, having done none for the entire week, Alfred feels a vague sense of apology. Mimi, quite equably, begins to clear the table. 'Just put it down, dear,' says Muriel, as Mimi prepares to dry the dishes which Muriel insists on washing herself. 'I'll just have a quiet moment with Ginger.' And she scoops up the enormous cat and buries her face in its fur. This quiet moment, complete with lavish endearments and innuendoes ('You appreciate me, don't you, sweetie, even if nobody else does') can last for some forty minutes, while Mimi stands politely with a tea-towel in her hand. When Mimi moves to the larder in an attempt to cover the rest of the food, Muriel says, 'Just put it down, dear,' and buries her face in the cat again. 'Well, Ginger,' she says eventually, 'I suppose I had better get the coffee ready.' And she does, too late, so that it keeps them all awake.

After dinner, Alfred goes out for a last walk round his domain. In the cool spring evening, he attempts to persuade himself that this is what he wants. As darkness falls, he strides up the little hills, with his imaginary dogs at his heels. In some recess of his being he knows that this is all wrong. He is aware that the inhabitants of the bungalows are watching him curiously out of their windows. He knows that back at Wren House Muriel will be heaving herself to her feet with a loud sigh and asking if anyone wants anything else before she puts her weary bones to bed. It should be all right but it is not, and Alfred begins to think that now it never will be. Oblivious to the indigo sky and the little twisted trees, Alfred strides on. In what glade, in what grove, can Alfred find his peace?

N I N E

ALFRED'S OTHER arrangements are a little more obscure.

Sitting in the garden of Wren House, with straight back, and wearing a paisley silk dress, Sofka tries to reconcile herself to the fact that Alfred no longer tells her everything. Like most mothers, she has forgotten that he never did tell her everything; what she means is that she is excluded from a part of his emotional life about which she would like to ask many questions. Why is he so late home in the week? Why does he invite so few friends to meet her? Why, above all, has he suddenly shot off in the car, after announcing that there will be two extra guests for lunch? They must be very important if he has taken the risk of upsetting Muriel in this daring manner. It is Muriel's lamentations which have driven Sofka out into the garden, while kind Mimi is attempting to help in the kitchen. And that is another cause for complaint: why does Mimi abase herself in this way? It is not as if she were unused to servants; the least she can do is to behave properly. Sofka is unmoved by the generous spirit thus shown. She is too offended by what she has seen of Muriel's domain to want her daughter to have any part of it. And now she knows that a punitive air will reign over the lunch, and she is too loving a mother not to grieve for Alfred, whose pleasure might thus be spoiled and who might be humiliated in front of his guests.

She is therefore all the more relieved when Alfred's guests turn out to be known to her after all. The aroma of gardenia stealing up this Kentish lane alerts her to the fact that one of these visitors can be none other than Dolly (Dorothea) who was once so very keen on Frederick and who was only just beaten to the post by Evie. In common with most of Frederick's former girlfriends, Dolly married shortly after his disappearance and chose from among her many suitors the one who bore the least resemblance to Frederick: Hal is a small dry man who is something important at the Board of Trade. The marriage, Sofka remembers, caused some surprise. Not that Hal is anything but a splendid character; he is certainly that and more. But he is very plain. The marriage, as it were, gave offence on aesthetic grounds. For Dolly is a great beauty, and always was. Dolly is the half-sister of Nettie, the little cousin of whom Alfred was so fond as a child. Nettie also married a plain man, but unlike Dolly she seems quite content. Not that she is very closely in touch these days; she seems to be busy all the time. Although neither sister has any children, and thus, one would think, plenty of opportunity to get in touch with their aunt by marriage.

Dolly, in fact, chose her husband for two reasons. One was his plainness, which sets off her extraordinary colouring. The other was his unobtrusive indulgence. Hal can refuse Dolly nothing, which is fortunate, because she lays claim to a great deal. Not only is she spoilt in the way of material adornment, which is her rightful due, after all, but she is, and this is rather more important, allowed to behave in a petulant and selfish manner which was originally thought to be adorable and which is now perhaps only a more exotic version of Nettie's high spirits. Dolly is one of those beauties whose beauty is their only justification. Her mahogany-coloured hair sets off her white face, which is a perfect oval, and her green eyes are rayed with lashes like the petals of a flower. Never mind her petulance and her imperious manners; she has always been like that, and anyway the women of this family seem to have these traits in common. Dolly causes a certain lack of jealousy by being so deliberately a chip off the old block. In a way the family has been proud of Dolly for being so irreducible, for being so majestic and impenitent a version of themselves.

Sofka is fond of Dolly, although she never thought her good enough for Frederick. Sofka appreciates her extravagant good looks, her self-indulgence, her exquisite appearance, and the dense aroma of gardenia with which she always surrounds herself, and which is even now commingling with the odour of roasting meat flowing out into the garden through the open kitchen door. Frederick always referred to Dolly as the Lady of the Gardenias and found her too sharp-tempered for his taste. Well, Dolly is sharp-tempered; there is no doubt of that. She is also liable to give offence, although always claiming that the other person is in the wrong. This is where Hal comes in. The deep complicity of their marriage is due to Hal's ability to absorb Dolly's permanent sense of having been wronged. Perhaps this feeling dates from Frederick's having chosen Evie, whose name Dolly has never ceased to blacken. Whatever the cause, it has made Dolly into a discontented woman who is allowed to express her discontent rather freely. The very real discontent beneath the disparaging manner is Hal's responsibility and one which he has assumed as part of his love for her. Hal will give his consent to anything as long as it assuages Dolly's fear that she is not being accorded her due.

Strange that such a beautiful woman can be so uncomfortable a companion! After embracing Sofka, Dolly is invited to join her on the lawn, but she can find no chair to her liking; they are all horrible, she claims, and a wicker footstool is kicked out of the way in Dolly's impatience to rearrange the circle to suit herself. Then the chair that Alfred brings out from the house is too low for her, and Hal is dispatched to look for something better. Alerted by this commotion, Mimi emerges from the back door, and is delighted to see her cousin, whom she has always admired. 'Mimi! What a sight you look,' says Dolly crossly, for she cannot bear to see another woman looking less than her best. 'Mimi has not been well,' Sofka murmurs, a little offended. 'Come and join us, darling,' she adds, with the tiniest note of pleading in her voice. 'I was just helping Muriel,' Mimi explains, referring to the apron she is wearing. 'And who is Muriel?' asks Dolly, although she knows perfectly well. Since Muriel has not been there to greet her, she has decided not to recognize her existence. 'Muriel takes care of us all,' says Alfred with some constraint, aware that Muriel is within earshot. 'I'm delighted to hear it,' pronounces Dolly. 'In that case I should like some coffee.'

Matters improve when Alfred takes Hal off for a tour of the estate, and Dolly expresses her blank amazement, her unfettered astonishment, at the mere fact of Muriel's existence. Dolly's meticulous grooming has always extended to every facet of her physical life, and the appearance of Muriel, in her blouse and her trousers, has stunned her but has not stunned her into wordlessness. Within minutes Mimi has collapsed into agonized laughter, and her mother is so relieved to see her behaving in this way that she allows herself a small smile of complicity, which flowers from time to time into a little laugh. Thus the three women are united and Dolly has fulfilled the family's expectations by being the only one brave enough to deplore Muriel's hegemony and the only one rude enough to criticize her appearance. It should be said at this point that Dolly is dressed for her day in the country in immaculate cream tussore, with a jade-green silk scarf to match her eyes. Sofka notices with a pang that there is a slight resemblance to her younger daughter Betty: that recessive gene that ordains seductive eyes and a sharp expression has emerged in Betty and in the two half-sisters, Dolly and Nettie, but has altogether missed Mimi and the boys. And Sofka sees that it is this recessive gene that leavens the ordinary good behaviour of this family; it is the enabling factor that points the way to will and to satisfaction.

Unfortunately, there can be little doubt that Alfred is in love with Dolly, a fact which Dolly chooses to exhibit and the rest to ignore. Hal's face and manner become drier and more impassive by the minute as Dolly teases Alfred; it is a sign of Alfred's lack of experience with women that he appears to be flattered by this. Sofka sighs, seeing merely that Dolly is living up to her reputation for bad behaviour. She fails to see, perhaps because she does not want to, that her son is involved in this bad behaviour. Mimi is uncomfortable; in fact, she is more than uncomfortable, she is frightened. Dolly's annexation of Alfred, in full view of her husband, brings to Mimi's mind unwanted reminiscences of that other annexation so long ago. Time has not eroded the horror of that episode, and Mimi has, rightly or wrongly, faced up to her disgrace ever since. It has made her fearful, apologetic, unable to try again. So that the sight of Dolly, who made her laugh so much before lunch and who is in some ways such an essential member of the family, turning into the sort of cruel and greedy woman of fickle appetites and steadfast self-regard whom Mimi has always feared has induced so much discomfort that she can feel a migraine starting and is forced to lie down. From her bedroom Mimi can hear their laughter: Dolly's and Alfred's. She can also hear the silence of Hal, and of Sofka.

It is wrong to suppose that Mimi does not notice these things. She notices them all too sharply. It is only by practising the strictest discipline on herself that she manages to think well of everyone else. All too often it seems to her that the world is a jungle, filled with humans no less rapacious than the animals. Were she to pursue her suspicions, or even to allow them to surface into consciousness, Mimi would be heartbroken. It is in order to avoid heartbreak that Mimi wills herself into accepting everything at face value. Thus Sofka is to her a mother whose love has never wavered, Alfred the brother whose noble self-sacrifice for his family has never been less than voluntary, Frederick a joy, and Betty an amusement. In this way Mimi arrives at the conclusion that Muriel's manners may be a little uncouth but that her heart is in the right place. And Dolly, well, Dolly is so beautiful that one can hardly expect her to conform to the rules that govern lesser people. In fact Mimi is well aware of danger in the present situation, and the headache is caused by her instinctive recognition that Alfred is no match for Dolly, that Dolly is paying off an old score, and that Hal will remain silent as this little drama is played out. Mimi feels for Alfred that identification of the victim for the potential victim; her heart grieves for him and also for her mother who seems a little bewildered by the childishness which has overtaken her younger son, he who has given so little evidence of childishness for more years than she cares to remember. By facing the truth, even momentarily, Mimi allows herself to think that, after all, they are grown up now, and with a tired sense of powerlessness she gets up and washes her face, and with some lessening of her symptoms, goes down to tea.

To suppose that those who are sexually inactive are also sexually inarticulate is a grave mistake, but one which is made with disheartening frequency. It would no doubt surprise Frederick, and also Betty, to know that Alfred has been, for some time now, activated into a sense of high tension by that aroma of gardenia, that he has chronicled every lapse of taste, every undeserved complaint, every show of temper that make up Dolly's usual style of behaviour, and that by watching them he has come to possess a very accurate knowledge of Dolly's style in other matters. Because of his former blamelessness, Alfred grants himself this descent, and already, in his mind, he commits acts whose daring would surprise all those who know him. Mimi is aware of all this. But she refuses to allow herself to become aware of the fact that these acts may not have been committed solely in the mind. Dolly is too beautiful and Alfred too handsome to permit her to contemplate them in full innocence. But it is the innocence of family life, under the eye of the matriarch, that Mimi accepts as being the only truth which she can bear to contemplate.

As for Alfred, whose sense of his destiny has begun to elude him, it would be asking of him too much to expect him to repudiate Dolly. What Alfred has been seeking, this long time, has been a badge of affinity between himself and the rest of the world. So much good behaviour has been visited upon him that he has felt himself becoming dull, neuter, destroyed as an independent being. He thought to preserve his ideals throughout his mother's lifetime; he thought to project them into the discovery or the creation of a mythic domain, where they would rest in amity like creatures in a better world. But the world, in the shape of Dolly, has been too much for him, and that house at the end of a long vista, with the smoke curling out of the chimneys and the golden dogs on the lawn, has been replaced by this duller reality in which Muriel is the reigning spirit, if spirit is not too discarnate a word. Alfred recognizes that he has reached that point in his life when his appetites will be made either risible or entirely valid. The fact that Hal is present, and a witness, is brushed aside. For once Alfred is determined to have his own way. His ideals have failed him, but his will remains.

To see Dolly and Alfred wandering slowly, side by side, up the lane by the side of Wren House, as Mimi sees them much later from her window, is to see complicity. To be sure, Alfred gestures occasionally at the scenery as if to indicate to any chance passer-by the normality of such wanderings, and no doubt his conversation is entirely factual, for Alfred, being what he is, has acquired more land, and has turned the place into a model farm. His initial investment is already showing a profit. In this placid landscape, Dolly, the Lady of the Gardenias, is monstrously unassimilable. In the drawing-room, Hal glances unobtrusively at his watch, computing some timetable of his own. 'Yes,' says Sofka, who has followed his glance. 'You will be wanting to get back. It is too bad of Alfred to set out on a walk just now. But I think the country is at its best in the early evening.' Sofka has quite enjoyed her day: she has enjoyed sitting and talking with Hal. In a way they make a compatible couple. It is almost as if Hal were in the same category of indulgent seniority as herself. Sofka gets up and goes to the window. 'I think I see them,' she tells Hal. 'I think I see Dolly's white dress.' But the dress disappears again into a clump of trees, and after a while Sofka sits down with Hal, and asks him if he would like more coffee.

When Dolly and Alfred return, their appearance is mildly shocking. Both, of course, are immaculate, undisturbed, but their eyes mirror the darkness of the night which seems to have fallen quite suddenly. Dolly disappears to make ready for the journey home, and in her absence Alfred is seen to laugh with a carelessness that is unfamiliar. It is as if Alfred has glimpsed a promised land, a land filled not only with Dolly but with the enactment of his own desires. That is what is so shocking about Alfred's appearance: he has lost his composure, his gravity. In their place there is a curious hilarity; he has never looked so young. He has ceased, almost in an instant, to observe the wishes of other people; he has thrown over all his careful upbringing; he is reconciled with the prospect of behaving in dubious taste. When an aroma of gardenia precedes the reappearance of Dolly, her jade silk scarf wound beautifully around her luminous face, Alfred takes one look at her, then turns to Hal, and says, 'But you can't go yet. There's no point in leaving now. If you wait an hour or two the roads will be absolutely empty.' Sofka, rather tired at this point, but rejoicing in her son's new exuberance, murmurs that perhaps Hal, who has a long drive in front of him, would rather leave now than later. 'Nonsense,' cries Alfred, who seems unwilling to let his visitors depart. 'You'll stay here and have an early dinner. I'll just tell Muriel.'

The fact that he will tell Muriel rather than ask her is but another sign of Alfred's emancipation. Needless to say, Muriel is not pleased, since she produced smoked salmon sandwiches at an hour which she thought would obviate the opportunity of dinner for the travellers. 'I can't start cooking now,' she says flatly. 'You'll have to have scrambled eggs.' 'Leave it to me,' says Dolly, unwinding her scarf. 'Hal swears by my scrambled eggs.' Hal looks at her with the veiled gaze of one who never swears at or by anything but is perhaps too dignified to intervene. Grumbling, Muriel follows Dolly into the kitchen in an attempt to forestall her. 'Is this where you keep the eggs?' Dolly can be heard to say. 'How quaint.'

It is not a comfortable meal but it is the one that Alfred

enjoys the most since he has presided over his own table. It is not even very speedily produced, for Dolly has rejected the sturdy pottery which Muriel thinks suitable for an impromptu supper, and has insisted on going through the many spacious cupboards in search of something more pleasing. Mimi, who has reappeared in order to see them off, and who still looks slightly blinded by her headache, is set to washing the fine china which Dolly has unearthed, while Muriel is instructed to throw away the tea-towels with which she liberally covers every surface and to go up to the linen cupboard and unpack some new ones. Suddenly the spirit of improvidence descends on the place, and is found to be rather heartening. Even Sofka laughs and takes a tea-towel. 'These spoons, Alfred. They came from my mother, you know. They need polishing.' 'Muriel will do them tomorrow,' says Alfred fearlessly. Muriel says nothing.

The table at last begins to resemble those virtuous and rewarding tables that Alfred has read about in the works of Charles Dickens. Dolly has even begun to behave like a niece. 'Sit down, Tanti,' she instructs Sofka, and Sofka smiles; it is like having Betty at home again. Mimi, with one hand shading her left eye, tries not to see too much with her right eye. And yet the scene is innocent. Even Hal is smiling. Alfred roars with appreciation as Dolly enters with a platter of eggs and toast. Tea is poured from a newly discovered Georgian teapot, which Muriel had placed out of reach on a high shelf because she does not want to polish it. Laughter rings out; family reminiscences are exchanged. And Dolly seems, in some way that none of them cares to examine, to have assumed her rightful place at the head of the table. Never mind Mimi, now trying not to wince at the noise; never mind Sofka, who has in any case always insisted on sitting at the foot; never mind Muriel, who hovers by the door quite mute with indignation; never mind Hal, who is so good-natured that he will sit anywhere. Never mind anyone, thinks Alfred, looking at Dolly; she is here, and I am here, and we are here in my house.

It is with the conviction that he has reached a watershed that Alfred allows himself to be so joyous. He has the mistaken impression that all those present both understand and forgive his behaviour. This is by no means the case. This air of family unity serves to disguise the unforgivable facts; for it is as a family that they are united and it is as a family that they will be disunited. The connection between Dolly and Alfred must not be examined: the taboos of the old world still obtain. And if Alfred, in his new spirit of liberation, and Dolly, in her old spirit of self-regard, are quite comfortable in this atmosphere, there are those present who are not. Mimi begins to think, quite uncharacteristically, that unless Dolly and Alfred treat Sofka with more deference they are in danger of courting her disapproval. Mimi knows that Sofka, as yet, suspects nothing, but that she will be alert to any dropping of standards. What Hal thinks nobody knows. Sofka is so tired by now that she remembers that Dolly always had a tendency to go too far and lets her mind drift back to the old days when Dolly and Nettie were children, when her children were children. And Muriel, who sees exactly what is happening, and who, moreover, sees what has happened, thinks that in future she might as well make herself pleasant to Dolly, because Dolly is the one who really counts in this place.

It is after supper, and rather late, that things begin to go a bit wrong. Dolly is so enlivened by her success that she fails to relinquish her position as head of the household. Is it by accident that she moves instinctively to Sofka's chair? Instinctively, Alfred and Mimi indicate another. This displeases Dolly who announces that she

really does not feel like going home yet, and that she would like a brandy. Brandy is produced, and for the sake of good form they are all given a little glass. It is not usual, thinks Sofka; what is different? She is now so tired that she would willingly go up with Mimi and leave them all, but it would not be polite. Yet she feels that Alfred should have noticed the signals and that he should have ensured that the house be quiet at this hour. 'Which way did you come down?' she asks Hal. 'It usually takes two hours when Alfred drives.' 'A little more than that,' says Hal, apparently without emotion. 'Come on, Dolly. Time we were going.' 'I want another brandy,' says Dolly.

It is at this point, seeing her son's rapt face, that Sofka gets to her feet. 'You will excuse me,' she says. 'I seem to tire so easily these days.' And it is true. Suddenly she can hardly climb the stairs. She looks in on Mimi and sees her sitting at the window, already in her nightgown, staring at the dark shape of the hill. This eruption of sexual energy has left Mimi thoughtful and despairing. By common consent, mother and daughter say nothing, but Sofka, despite her tiredness, sits for a while, with her cool dry hand stroking Mimi's brow. Then she leads her to the bed, and sits with her again, as if Mimi were still a child and the two of them were still in the old nursery. When she judges Mimi to be asleep, she gets stiffly to her feet, goes to her room, and closes the door, unwilling to catch a thread of noise from downstairs. As she lies, apparently composed, in her plain lawn nightgown, she hears Muriel clump up to bed. Then, very late, she hears the car drive off, and the doors being bolted. Finally she hears Alfred, whose steps seem to be furtive, but who is simply trying not to make a noise, going past her and into his room.

Well, thinks Sofka, he is a man now. He is not the boy who longed for my hand on his brow when he had been reading too much, and who whispered to me at the table, safe by my side. He is a man and he is doing important work; he must have his flirtations like other men. Had it been Frederick, the thought would have given her pleasure; as it is Alfred, she feels pain. I had hoped to keep him with me, my true son, and now my son is turning into his father's son. And with Dolly! I remember them as children, laughing and over-excited. I never thought he would marry, like the others. I thought he had passed the age of danger.

The hours of the night seem very long and very slow; it is as though the significance of this day cannot easily be relinquished. Sofka does not sleep, but addresses the Almighty, rather as she would address her bank manager, with the assurance of one who has always been solvent. I have loved them, she assures the deity in whom she does not fully believe. I think they have loved me. I am tired now. All I ask is that I should keep them a little longer. There will be time later. If Alfred is to make a fool of himself, at least let him avoid bringing disgrace on the family. You know that I have done my best. I have kept the faith. Please let Alfred settle for an *affaire* rather than insist on a divorce. That is what my husband always did, and everybody seemed to like him for it. I really do not understand these matters. Please let Alfred stay with me. If I am to lose anyone, let it not be Alfred. The best solution would be for Mimi to find a good man and marry him. Alfred would not then leave me alone. You know that I am getting old. I do not know how long I have left. I have not asked for much, but all in all I have been grateful. I only ask for Alfred's sake. He has always been so good. And it would be a pity if he were to change.

As the house settles down and the night slips into the next day, a cool wind springs up and stirs the curtains. Sofka takes this as a sign that her message has been received, and at last allows herself to sleep.

T E N

As the weather turns cold and the year slips into darkness, fewer weekends are spent at Wren House. There seems to be a tacit agreement about this on both sides. Sofka prefers, or says she prefers, the warmth of the flat in Bryanston Square; Alfred explains that it is not fair to Muriel to expect her to house and feed his guests every weekend. At this, Sofka raises an eyebrow, but says nothing. She has no wish to know what happens at Wren House these days. She is more at ease in the dark and familiar confines of her cigar-coloured drawing-room, with its brown velvet curtains shuttered against the night. She has taken to sitting there for most of the day now, paying fewer visits to the girls in the kitchen, no longer interested in the clothes they make for themselves, or the boyfriends they treat so cruelly and with so much laughter. Sometimes she will sit for a long time listening to Mimi's piano ('*O doux printemps d'autrefois . . .*') and her hand will begin to shake. 'Mimi,' she says. 'Why don't you sing that song that Betty used to sing? "*Les Filles de Cadiz*", it was called. Betty sang it so beautifully.' I shall never see her again, she thinks. She is too far away.

Sometimes, to please her, Mimi sings the song, but it does not sound the same. Mimi's voice is too veiled, too elegiac, too devoid of Betty's snap and vivacity. She makes the invitation in the song sound implausible, unconvincing, in poor taste: a failed attempt. At thirty-five Mimi seems unfledged. As a young girl she had been enchanting; her innocence was then reflected in the candour of her looks. The heavy hair, the smile of greeting, the hesitant walk may not have been conventionally attractive; but, more important, they were disarming. One looked and saw no guile. There is still no guile in Mimi, and Sofka almost wishes that there were. She compares Mimi's silent presence in the apartment with the girls and their irruptions. 'Madam, Madam, Mrs Sofka, darling! What do you think? With earrings or without? All right for his family, yes? As if I care!' And they flounce away, fortified by the courage of their own intentions. These girls are sensible, even wise. They know that when Sofka dies, or sooner, they will have to leave the safety of this house and find another. Therefore they intend to secure husbands, whom they will intrigue and who will provide for them, and provide lavishly. There is no sentiment here. Lili and Ursie have discarded sentiment as a luxury, and one which might prove bad for their looks. How Sofka admires them for this! Her own life has been spent in avoidance of the fatal passion and she has not, she thinks, been wrong. She knows nothing of that voluptuous flight from the contingencies of normal living, that surrender of the will, that rich harvest of inner thought and memory. She knows only what is appropriate, suitable, in order. She knows that possession of a husband confers status on a woman, and if that status is undeserved, what of that? Sofka knows, and she is right, that nothing is worth waiting for, not even the ideal partner, not even if that ideal partner exists. Sofka knows that a woman of thirty-five without a husband is to be pitied, and is indeed pitied by those who ignore her essence and who will almost certainly denigrate her virtues.

This question of Mimi's future preoccupies Sofka these days, almost to the exclusion of considerations of Alfred's arrangements. Perhaps she concentrates on Mimi so as not to worry about what is happening at Wren House and indeed at Hyde Park Street, home of Hal and Dolly. The year seems colder to her than previous years and she becomes a little agitated as night comes on. Well, she is no longer young, she reminds herself. It is natural for her to feel anxiety for the children that are left.

Of Mimi's inner landscape she has little idea, focusing her attention on Mimi's appearance which does indeed begin to reflect that dereliction of spirit that has overtaken Mimi in recent years. She does not know, for example, of Mimi's profound despair, which proceeds from a sense of exclusion from the living world. Unlike Alfred, Mimi has been too long disabled to fight her way clear. The enactment of Mimi's desires is all retrospective, in the mind. Mimi constantly rewrites the script that decreed that she should remain solitary that night in the Hôtel Bedford et West End. It is not Frank for whom she yearns now but for that missing factor in herself that would have brought Frank to her side. She blames herself entirely for this omission, and maybe she is right. Somehow she knows, correctly, that without this false start, this disgrace, this defeat, she could have taken her chance like any other woman. But since that morning when, dry-mouthed and dry-eyed, she got up and dressed herself and left the hotel, she no longer feels a part of her time, of her age: she feels invisible. It is as much as she can do now to avoid pain, simply to avoid pain. Therefore, this nun-like existence with her mother and her brother, these afternoons lying down and nursing a headache, this unalterably serene service at the hospital, enable her to get through the day as quickly and as quietly as possible and prepare the way for the night, which is her own time.

For then she thinks entirely, exclusively, of herself. She does not ask what is to become of her. She knows. She will stay here in this apartment, with Sofka, and intermittently with Alfred, and she will pursue this unabrasive way of life until death takes her. In this way she will remain true to herself. For passionate souls, it has been truly remarked, do not find friendship easy. And, it might have been added, nor love either, after a certain time.

The days pass, unvariegated. Mother and daughter sit at table. There is very little for either of them to do. The only sounds come from the kitchen, where Lili and Ursie cry less these days and laugh more. Nobody is ill. Nobody is poor. Indeed they are rather rich. Alfred joins them two or three times a week, when business or pleasure can spare him, and they do not enquire of him what he is doing. Pleasing concern for his health is all that is expressed, which is just as well, because Alfred is testy and authoritative these days: his temper is uncertain, and mother and daughter gently suggest that he is working too hard. The polite convention is that it is Alfred's work that sometimes keeps him away at night. And by common consent, it is the cares and burdens of a man of affairs, a man of property, that they all deplore. Alfred is quite willing to subscribe to this convention, which is not entirely a fiction. He is indeed burdened these days.

'Alfred,' says Sofka. 'You have hardly touched your dessert.' It is a vanilla cream, one of his favourites. She puts in front of him the silver bonbonnière filled with almonds and muscatels. He looks at it blankly, then pushes it away. 'Not hungry, Mama. Tell Lili to bring me some coffee in the study. I have some papers to go through.' The study is where the telephone is.

'But Alfred,' protests Sofka gently. 'Why not let Lautner . . . ?'

'Lautner is useless,' says Alfred, rather harshly, but he is anxious to be gone.

How is Lautner these days? He is in fact far from useless: he is indispensable. Not only is he the agent whereby certain monies are paid regularly to Mrs Beck and her kind; not only does he know the work of the factory by heart; not only is he acquainted with the business of the household and its expenses; not only has he made arrangements, as instructed, for dowries for Lili and Ursie; because of all this, because, too, of his dull decency, his unfailing rectitude, Lautner is the repository of the family's secrets and its link with the past. From his flat in Kentish Town which he has never sought to improve, Lautner still presents himself, on Sundays, to take coffee and marzipan cake, although these days he is mostly served in the kitchen. He has been very kind to the girls, Lili and Ursie, has brought them little bouquets of flowers which they put carelessly into vases. Nevertheless he thinks well of these girls, whose arrival he was instructed to organize, whom he has comforted in their initial distress, and whom he knows to be part of the family, which is the only family he has now. Once Sofka sounded the girls as to what they felt about Lautner, but they simply looked at each other and burst out laughing. And it is true that Lautner, in his old-fashioned suits, and with the watch that he checks against every clock that he encounters, would not be suitable for the girls. 'He is too old!' they protest. 'Mrs Sofka, darling, he is nearly sixty!' 'He is fifty-nine,' Sofka reproves them. 'And he is the salt of the earth.' But they remain unconvinced. What is the salt of the earth to them? They do not even understand the expression.

When Lautner next comes to Bryanston Square, Sofka sends word that he is to join her in the drawing-room. She has dressed herself in her grey silk, as she sometimes does on a Sunday, and she would dearly love a little company, feeling brighter that day and somewhat cheered by the late autumn sunshine.

'Sit down, Joseph,' she says. 'It is many Sundays since we had a talk.' And she indicates a chair on the other side of the coffee-table and prepares to cut the marzipan cake. 'And it is time I called you Joseph, is it not?'

'Indeed, Mrs Dorn, I am only too happy . . . '

Lautner is indeed happy at this attention. He has begun to wonder recently how he will fill his days when Alfred suggests that he retire, as he rather suspects that Alfred has a mind to do. Alfred is a hard task-master, unlike Frederick, whose inspired comings and goings enlivened Lautner, made him feel necessary, indulgent, responsible. Oddly enough, Lautner was by no means impervious to the romance of Frederick's life. Like most men without a family he has espoused the family to which he does not belong with total acceptance and complete devotion. Alfred is more difficult to get along with than his brother ever was. He has a harsher manner. Frederick was more like his father, Lautner reflects. But Alfred is a better businessman, a better financier than Frederick could ever have been. So excellent is Alfred in these respects that Lautner no longer finds himself as necessary as he did previously, and sometimes he has to serve in a quite subordinate capacity.

'What news of the children, Mrs Dorn?' he asks, after the usual enquiries about her health. For to Lautner, as to Sofka, they are still the children.

Sofka smiles. 'Frederick and Evie are coming home for a visit soon,' she says. 'Just think! I haven't seen him since before the war! And he has two children now, twins.' But privately she does not think much of these twins, of whom she has seen photographs. They are squarish children, the image of their mother, with all their mother's teeth. They are called Erica and Thomas, uninteresting names. Sofka does not think of shortening these names, for in some way she feels that the twins have nothing to do with the family to which she belongs. And the Frederick she remembers so vividly had nothing of a father about him.

'And Betty is in Hollywood! Just think! Her husband makes films for television, and Betty has her own swimming pool. Alfred has promised to take me to see her one day. But I don't think I shall go. I am getting old, Joseph.' She sighs. Lautner is moved; greatly daring, he puts his hand on hers. Sofka smiles. 'Of course, Betty writes. It is all going so well for them. And sometimes she sends a parcel of clothes for Mimi. But they don't fit her. And they wouldn't suit her even if they did. Betty was a gipsy. My gipsy.' She smiles again.

'And Miss Mimi?' Lautner asks.

Sofka sighs. 'I worry about her,' she says. And the animation leaves her face.

When Mimi comes in for coffee, she is surprised to find Lautner still there, for he usually stays only half an hour or so. She wonders what her mother can have found to talk to him about this long time. But she appreciates the way he stands up and arranges her chair and hands over her coffee-cup. She has always liked his careful manners and his respectful devotion to her mother. And she has known him for so long – since she was a child, in fact – that she hardly thinks of him as a man. More of a background, a shade.

'Do you still go to concerts, as you used to, Joseph?' enquires Sofka.

'Indeed, Mrs Dorn, indeed. I have tickets for a piano recital at the Wigmore Hall this Wednesday. I know that Miss Mimi is fond of the piano. I used to hear her playing, years ago, when I came to the house. I wonder . . . ' He turns to her. 'I wonder, Miss Mimi, would you by any chance be free?'

Mimi hesitates, as she always does when she receives an invitation, searching vainly for an excuse.

He smiles at her, as if reading her mind.

'It will be for two hours only. I will collect you and bring you back immediately afterwards, and you will have heard a good programme of your beloved Chopin.'

Mimi assents weakly, rather surprised that her mother will permit this. It has never happened before, and she sees no reason why it should happen now. But as she sees Sofka and Lautner smiling at her with such affection, she supposes that for once it will be only polite not to disappoint them.

And so it is arranged. Just what is arranged is imprecise but is understood by both Sofka and Lautner. There could be no more delicate suitor than Joseph Lautner. Sometimes a concert, more often a long walk on Sunday afternoon before returning to Bryanston Square and to Sofka. So delicate a suitor is Lautner that Mimi has no idea of his intentions. She is however rather encouraged by his self-effacing company, and when he offers her his arm, during those gentle walks through Regent's Park, she takes it unhesitatingly, feeling him to be the father, the protector, that she lost too soon. There is no doubt that her headaches have improved and her appearance has benefited from the fresh air, the exercise, and even the company. No longer does she spend disheartening Sundays in her bedroom, trying on the vivid flimsy clothes that Betty sends, and seeing that they make her look sallow, thin, and old. Her good tweed suit and her walking shoes are all that is required of her. And how anxious Lautner is that she should be warm enough! And how carefully he reassures Sofka that they will be back in two hours, two and a half at the most! 'Joseph, Joseph,' smiles

Sofka. 'I know that she is safe with you.' And indeed she is.

But Mimi, because she feels nothing but a mild reassurance and none of that sense of failed destiny that has dogged her, has indeed ruined her life, has no idea what is going on. For Mimi, these walks, these concerts, are simply, like everything else, ways of passing the time. And these little excursions are never discussed, as, Mimi supposes, more significant encounters are discussed between mother and daughter. And by common consent they are never referred to in front of Alfred who regards Lautner's attendance with only barely concealed irritation. 'Are you keeping your swain in good order, Mimi?' he demands with a laugh. Yet there is ferocity in the laugh, as if something preposterous is going on and should not be allowed to continue. As if he will disbar Lautner, with a few unmistakable words, should the need arise. Therefore Lautner's visits are not much discussed at Bryanston Square.

When Lautner, after a few words to Sofka behind the closed door of the drawing-room, asks Mimi to marry him she immediately retreats to her room with a headache. Strange; she has not had one for some time. And this one is quite severe, complicated as it is by tears of anguish. Destiny, which failed Mimi once, seems about to do so again. For she knows, instinctively, that she was meant to be the wife of a man so inevitably, so truly loved that he would validate her entire existence. And that without such a love she will remain invalid, insignificant, and, worse, disabused. 'Send him away, Mama,' she begs, when her mother comes later into her room. 'I cannot marry him. It is impossible.'

Sofka enters the room and shuts the door behind her. 'He has gone,' she assures Mimi drily. 'Did you think he was waiting for your answer, cap in hand? He is not a peasant, you know. He is a man.' The distinction is quite clear to her.

'It is no good, Mama. I don't love him and I never shall. He is the man who used to wait in the hall, down below, when Betty and I were young.' And she passes a weary hand over her aching brow. 'I don't want to see him again. Tell him not to come back.'

'Mimi,' says Sofka. 'You talk like a child. How should I send Lautner away? He has been coming to the house since Papa died. He is almost part of the family. And he has his pride, you know. In fact, he has more than you have. Look at you! Your eyes are red, your hair is untidy. And when you receive a proposal of marriage, you cry like a baby. What kind of behaviour is this?'

Mimi bows her head. 'It is because I don't love him,' she whispers. She has never touched on these matters before and is anxious to avoid them now.

'Love!' says Sofka scornfully. 'It is marriage we are talking about. He does not ask you to love him. He asks you to care for him as he will care for you. You have enjoyed his company, the concerts, the walks. He knows your ways, our ways. That is what matters, believe me. And you are not getting any younger.'

'Mama,' begs Mimi. 'Leave me alone.'

'Daughter!' cries Sofka, in a loud voice which startles them both, as does the archaic use of the word. 'I do not want to die and leave you alone. I do not want you to remain my little child, without your mother to run to. Do you know what they say of such women? Do you know what it is like for a woman to grow old without a man? To be a godmother to other women's children, useful for presents and otherwise disregarded? Do you know what it is like never to set a family table? Never to celebrate? To sit alone, because it is inconvenient for your friends to invite you? Do you know what it is to be

133

left out of other people's plans? To be left out of their conversations, even? Do you want to grow old like this, playing the piano, dreaming like a girl? Do you know the names that other women apply to women like you?'

Mimi lifts her head and stares at her mother in horror.

'Do they talk about me, then?' she asks.

'Yes,' says Sofka. 'They talk about you. As if you had some fatal illness, which God forbid. But they will not talk about you after your wedding. Lautner is not undignified. He is a good man. And no one will talk about you in that way when they see your house, when they admire your possessions, when they come to your afternoons. Papa left you a settlement, you know. You will not be poor. And when you have a child of your own, then you will no longer be angry with your mother. Then, my darling, you will rejoice and be proud and be a real woman at last.'

There is silence. 'Trust me, Mimi,' says Sofka, smoothing the untidy hair. 'And show them, show your family, what you are made of. We have all waited a long time.'

'*You* have waited?' asks Mimi, with a strange laugh. 'Then I must not keep you waiting any longer.'

When Mimi sits down at the table for dinner, she is bathed, changed, and to all intents and purposes entirely calm. It so happens that Alfred is present that evening, and with the faintest touch of irony Mimi allows her mother to tell him the glad news. Alfred's response is explosive. 'You must both be mad,' he says. 'Lautner! Of all people! Lautner!'

'I think you had better practise calling him Joseph,' says Mimi, unmoved. 'I should like the wine sauce, if you please, Alfred. It is just by your elbow, as usual.'

Alfred looks stunned at this evidence of insubordination. His sister has always waited on him, deferred to his wishes, kept an anxious watch on his appetite. His sister has always been like his mother, in this respect. And here is his mother, looking down at her plate, trying to efface a smile, then looking up again with the expression of one contemplating vast and harmonious horizons, as if nothing were amiss.

'You can't get married,' explodes Alfred. 'You can't even cook. You don't know anything about running a house. And where are you going to live, by the way? Not here, I hope?' The prospect seems to stagger him. The idea of living on equal terms with Lautner makes a mockery of everything that he has worked for, his ruined childhood, his desiccated manhood, the freedom which he has had to renegotiate all the time, always on other people's terms, it seems to him.

'Joseph has a place in Kentish Town,' says Mimi calmly, emptying the jug of wine sauce over the square of batter pudding on her plate. 'I dare say that it will do until I can look around for something better.'

'Why not wait until you have found somewhere, darling?' murmurs Sofka, not really anxious to allow too much delay.

'Oh, no,' says Mimi. 'I should like to get married as soon as possible.'

'Lautner!' explodes Alfred once more, as the meal draws to a close. 'He used to brush my father's coat.'

'You may be quite sure that he will not brush yours, Alfred,' says Mimi, folding her napkin and pushing it through its silver ring. 'Will you ask for coffee, Mama, or shall I?'

In the weeks that follow, Mimi has a not unpleasant time spending a great deal of money. Even Sofka is rather surprised at the quantities of linen and china that Mimi decides she needs. Clothes are ordered from the dressmaker, and a fur coat is designed by Sofka's furrier. Sofka is briefly revived by all these acquisitions: she is also encouraged to see Mimi so purposeful. As the boxes and packages mount up in the flat she wonders whether there will be room for all these purchases in Kentish Town. Mimi does not appear to give this matter much consideration. 'What I don't need I will send for later,' she tells her mother. 'You can leave everything in my room for the present.' Dolly comes to tea, ready to disparage, but is forced to concede that the preparations are of high quality. Alfred spends as much time at Wren House as he can during these weeks of activity. He is not looking forward to the change, and congratulates himself on being able to escape at the weekends. Sometimes he makes the weekend stretch as far as Tuesday. After all, if Lautner is to be one of the family, there is no reason why he should not make himself as useful as possible.

The piano is silent these days. Mimi has not yet decided whether she will have it moved to Kentish Town. She seems to want to get away from the old image, the old memory of herself, sitting in her room, and dreaming, and passing the time as best she can. She has told them at the hospital that she will not be coming back for the time being, although she will keep in touch. They have given her a very pretty china cake-stand as a wedding present.

Here they all are in the photograph. Lautner looks radiant. Sofka wears a dress of parma violet, with a little hat of violet petals. (I have this on record.) Here are Nettie and Dolly, looking as unlike each other as it is possible for half-sisters to look. Strangely enough, those two have never got on very well. Dolly looks stunning, in a burnt orange two-piece. Nettie wears pale blue, which sets off her still beautiful hair. Hal is there, of course. And Nettie's funny little good-natured husband, Will, whom they see all too rarely. And the girls, Lili and Ursie, dressed to the nines and ogling the photographer. There are some absences, of course. Frederick and Evie have sent a telegram. 'Heartbroken not to be with you today. Love to our dearest Mimi.' And there is one from Betty, who is rather mercifully absent as well. 'Love and kisses to my big sister on her wedding day.' Mimi herself surprises them all by wearing white peau-de-soie and carrying a great many flowers; she looks extremely gracious, rather grand. After all, she is not her mother's daughter for nothing. Alfred, who gave her away, is very stern. Alfred's brow, in fact, is like thunder. Is that why Sofka has tucked a restraining hand through his arm?

E L E V E N

FREDERICK, becalmed in Bordighera, rarely thinks of home. The war, which isolated them all in this little town, seems to have cut them off definitively from their roots. The war, of course, was bad for business, but for Frederick and Evie it was a time of astonishing calm, even happiness. Both have proved themselves to be fearless and adaptable in the business of survival. As soon as they saw signs of invading patrols of any description they hastened down to the enormous cellar, the existence of which very few suspected, and emerged with several choice bottles in which they insisted on drinking their visitors' health. For this reason they were soon on friendly terms with officers of more than one nationality, for the wine was too good to bring to the notice of the common soldiery who would in any case merely have smashed the bottles. With fine vintages as their currency, Evie and Frederick obtained enough food to live on and were content with simple fare – sardines and cheese and olives and bread and fruit – which kept them healthy and bright-eyed in appearance. So welcoming were Evie and Frederick, with the hoteliers' knack of instant appreciation of the client's needs, that the officers would take to dropping in to the deserted hotel in the evenings for a bottle of wine and a little relaxation; parcels of comestibles would change hands, and, after a brief wordless nod from Evie,

Frederick would then proffer the fine cigars which he had saved from his father's belongings. Although war and depredation may have raged up and down the coast, all was peace and amity at the Hotel Windsor in Bordighera.

With so little to do and no guests to provide for, Evie and Frederick could concentrate more easily on each other. This war, which separated so many couples, merely reinforced their dependence on each other. It was with deep joy that they awaited the birth of their twins, attended only by the ancient village doctor, who delivered them in one of the spare rooms of the Hotel Windsor. Evie, up and about within five days, gave proof that the earthiness that first enslaved Frederick was in fact true currency: fecund and beaming, Evie found motherhood the easiest thing in the world. Slopping around in old sandals, her springy hair slipping from its moorings, she gave evidence of a profound sluttishness; Frederick remembers her face shining moistly, her spotless tongue slipping between her unpainted lips, her effortless and unselfconscious squatting as she cleaned up a little spilt milk or one of the dog's accidents. In fact, Evie found this wartime *déshabillé* so much to her liking that, once the bad times are past, and the hotel begins to fill up again, Frederick has some difficulty in persuading her to go to the hairdresser and the dressmaker and to put on stockings and lipstick. He will always think of the essential Evie as bare-legged, her feet in broken *savates*, her nightgown slightly soiled with milk, yawning and stretching in the early morning, and, half-asleep, going through to the dressing-room to feed the babies. Frederick, with the finely attuned senses of a man who has always loved women, finds this scene ravishing, voluptuous. Evie, who never really worried, knows that she will not lose him now.

Frederick's earlier friends would be a little surprised to

see him these days. He has put on quite a bit of weight, and his hair, now sleek and much longer, is peppered with grey. He wears cream linen trousers, a white cotton shirt, and a panama hat. Only the pale narrow shoes reveal the cad and the dandy that Frederick used to be. This uniform is unvarying. The hat is in place when Frederick enters the hotel lounge from his private quarters at nine o'clock every morning. He has already been to the station for the newspapers, which he places on the glass-topped wicker tables, and then he briefly takes a turn in the garden, where the gardener's hosepipe is playing on the tubs of orange-trees. After this he is more or less free until the evening, for Evie has wisely decided to treat him as if he were a boy, on holiday from school, which is exactly how Frederick feels. It is this odd mixture of juvenility and paunchy assiduity that would confound Frederick's earlier friends. In his panama hat and his pale shoes, his short-sleeved shirt, in the breast pocket of which his lunchtime cigar is visible, and the slightly fatuous smile of contentment on his face, Frederick seems as disarmed and as disarming as any innocent tourist. Frederick has always been a tourist rather than a traveller. He has no real interest in one place as against any other. He appears to see no differences in landscape or customs provided that his own comforts are assured and his habits safely accommodated. He accepts the Hotel Windsor as his home in much the same way that he once took his ease in his mother's house. A faintly patronal air was there from the start, and, by the same token, the good manners of the excellent guest that he always was. Frederick was the guest of his mother; rising from his chair in her drawing-room to welcome the friends who used to come for coffee and marzipan cake on a Sunday afternoon, he would have the same expansive and attentive air that he now uses to such good purpose in his new trade. What would puzzle his friends,

140

apart from Frederick's appearance, would be to see this process reversed, to see assiduity shading into automatic *bonhomie*, and the patron only taking his ease when the demands of the guests have been attended to.

Yet Frederick has no idea that a shift has taken place in both his fortunes and his reputation. This may be, of course, because there is no one around from the old days to witness the change. Is it perhaps for this reason that Frederick feels an instinctive reluctance towards the mere idea of going home for a visit? Does he know that this combination, so marvellously to his taste, of Evie's sluttishness and his own dandyish but decidedly foreign appearance, might not pass muster with his mother, his brother, under the weeping skies of London, a city which now appears to him as small, huddled, grey, and unheroic? By unheroic Frederick implies no moral failing; morals rarely come into his equations. In any event he has had no need of heroism himself; the cellars have furnished him with an easier means of exchange. No, by unheroic Frederick understands himself to mean dreary, lacking in expansion, lacking in physical excellence. Frederick, acute always to the implications of colour, outline, the elegance of silhouette, the charm of appearance, far prefers this little town, where, under skies as blue and as cloudless as the inside of a painted cup, he can stroll down the Corso Italia and see nothing less harmonious than the jagged leaves of an overgrown palm tree. Stepping delicately but briskly down the Corso on his way to the station, Frederick will see oranges and lemons growing on trees; he will see and smell the café with its gusts of vanilla and its squawking coffee machines; he will greet the spotless and handsome waiter opening up the restaurant for an airing before lunch; and he will wave to the old lady who keeps the ironmonger's and for whom he will sometimes take a letter to the post. In this way, the golden light that illuminates Frederick's early morning excursion will have effectively blotted out the sparse colour and harsh winds of London, where he feels he would no longer be at home. In any case, he knows that the old house has been sold and that the family has moved to Bryanston Square; it would hardly count as going home now even if he were to go back. Frederick feels that the family has moved away from him rather than the other way around. In any event, under the impact of this unvarying light, it is very difficult to imagine himself returning to anything less brilliant, less natural, less effortless than this place. Frederick, like any other instinctive creature, espouses a habitat where he is most at ease.

Of course, he will go home some day and see his mother; he has promised her as much. And of course she must see her grandchildren, his children, of whom he is immensely proud. In a way it would have been a good idea to go back for Mimi's wedding, the news of which came as a considerable surprise. But after happy days in his pale shoes and his panama hat Frederick cannot quite see himself in the solemnity of a morning coat and in a crush of relations. He really does not care for all those people any more: his mother and his sister he prefers to cherish as golden presences about his early youth, unmarked by age or care or change. He thinks it not a bad idea that Mimi should marry Lautner. They both, he sees, have some quality of gravity which makes them natural partners but with which he was never completely at ease. And he likes to think of an additional member of staff, as it were, on duty to care for his mother. In a way, it is as if Lautner were substituting for himself as he so often did in the past. Yes, he is all for the marriage, but as he sees it there is no longer any reason for him to be present. If Lautner is there then Frederick is relieved of his duties. He sends a telegram, of course, and treats himself to a cognac after lunch in which he drinks his sister's health.

Frederick's contacts with England are now confined to whatever Sofka and Mimi care to send. A constant stream of requests for Start-Rite shoes, Dundee marmalade, and Floris's New Mown Hay goes out from Bordighera to London and is answered by carefully packed parcels and letters of credit to a bank in Nice. Alfred has proved remarkably successful in business, as Frederick always knew that he would, and Frederick has no qualms in asking for some of the profits, for which, as he sees it, he is partly responsible. Besides, the hotel needs extra staff and the money has to come from somewhere; Evie's Dadda lost quite a bit in the war, and she feels that he deserves great sympathy in this respect; the funds in Switzerland are not to be drawn on until Dadda dies, and anyway that money will come to Evie. It is only right that this money should be balanced by something from the other side of the family. In this way Frederick manages to think of England as a place of funds and commodities, devoted to that business which he always disliked, and functioning as a service area for places of natural enchantment and superiority where lives may be more pleasantly and more attractively lived. If there is any hint of filial impiety from Alfred, whose letters are curt and without affection, Frederick has one unanswerable trump card: he has fathered twins. He is, of all Sofka's children, the only one who has gone forth and multiplied. There can be no criticism that will not be nullified by this evidence of fruitfulness. By this very act of fathering his children Frederick has placed himself beyond reproach.

And he loves these children, who so resemble their mother, and who, in response to their mother's excellent nurturing instinct, grew up without problems, without those little finicky appetites which had always dogged his brother and his sisters, without faces pale and temples hollowed by the hours of reading that he remembers as such a feature of his own youth. Frederick's children, Erica and Thomas, have always slept through the night and have eaten everything that is given to them. They enjoy scratched legs, dirty faces, and days in the open air; they flourish on the intermittent hygiene meted out by their mother, on the inappropriate menus which come down to them from the hotel dining-room, and from the ice-creams at the café for which Frederick always slips them money. Erica and Thomas speak Italian and a sort of French, both with lingering uneducated accents; they are sharp and resourceful children, and they will never be properly educated. In many ways they resemble the children of the environs; canny and quick and very slightly underhand. They will do well, and they will never go home. Yet, with their square teeth and their Start-Rite shoes, they grin convincingly enough in the photographs which Frederick sends home to his mother to set her murmuring about resemblances and peering at the tiny faces in an effort to see reflected there the image of her beloved son.

On this sunny morning, as on so many others, Frederick walks down the Corso Italia, turning his head from side to side the better to savour the varied delights that are brought to the attention of his senses: the smell of vanilla from the café, the hose playing about the orange-tree tubs in the garden, the pleasant bustle of early morning, and the impeccable sky of uninflected blue. Despite the charms of Bordighera, Frederick is making for Nice, as is his habit. If the car is not free he will take the train, which saves him a lot of trouble at the frontier even if it does take a little longer. He is usually in Nice by midday and he takes a taxi to the old town so that he can spend an hour in the market before sitting down to a pleasant lunch in any of half a dozen favourite places behind the harbour.

Frederick will rarely buy anything in the market but the place has become essential to him as a storehouse of further sights, smells, and impressions to feed his ever greedy sensorium. From the flower market, with its tightly furled bouquets of carnations – red, pink, white, yellow, striped, and even dyed blue – Frederick will penetrate to the inner secret depths of the old town. Here, on precipitously stepped and cobbled streets, twisting blindly and abruptly around corners and slippery with fish scales, Frederick will tread carefully in his pale shoes, tipping his hat to those stall holders who recognize him from previous visits. He will appreciate, with an equal and a discerning eye, a tuft of coarse grass thrusting up through the cobbles where the alley meets the wall of the church of St Rita, the butcher's boy emerging with uplifted hatchet from the back of the shop to check on the symmetry and the quantity of the day's display of lamb chops in white enamelled trays, the priest with his long soutane and his furled black hat, the basket of cheap but elegant shoes in the doorway of a shop so dark that it is necessary to put most of its goods on the pavement, the sharp and almost sickening smell of the cheeses laid out on leaves of fern and palm, the sudden gleam of a coffee machine and the spurt of its steam, the blessed sight of the fresh loaves of bread, newly baked for lunchtime, being set up vertically in the window of the baker's shop. Sometimes Frederick will imagine himself loading baskets with sticks of bread and portions of different paté – the rabbit, the goose, the hare – and bushels of mirabelle plums, and taking those baskets somewhere where he and Evie can steal away from the children and eat. But as he is on his own, Frederick puts his excellent sensual imagination to work and enjoys, vicariously, the delights which the shopkeepers and stall holders arrange for his delectation. Frederick is such a happy man, so elegant, so smiling, as he wends his way down the slippery and sharply descending streets, that everyone gives him a greeting; it hardly matters that he never buys anything, for he has become in a sense the spirit of the place, if not its patron, and merely to see him there in his pale shoes and his immaculate shirt and his panama hat is to receive a lift to the heart, as if this market, in which humbler people ply their trades, has been granted a certificate of excellence from the most enlightened of connoisseurs. Frederick raises his hat to old ladies in black who have slipped out for a cutlet and a bottle of wine and a baguette for their lunch; he notices the sinewy cats that weave figures of eight around the old ladies' slippered feet, and he empathetically imagines that he too is an old lady, free at last to please herself, to get fat, and let her feet go, and emerge from aromatic gloom to the dark blue sky above and the dusky smell of the cheese shop and the cool shape of the bottle in one's hand and the prospect of a long siesta. Frederick raises his hat to the priest, and, for courtesy's sake, enters the small hot gaudy church of St Rita and slips some money into the wooden box; sometimes he lights a tapering candle, for the sheer pleasure of seeing the flame reluctantly take hold and climb up the white unsullied wick and achieve a steady pale glow; he will sniff the incense with the same careful nose that he once laid to a cigar. Finally, he will take a small cup of black coffee standing at the counter of a dark café, a mere tunnel between two shops, glittering with the chrome of its coffee machine and alive with the cries and greeting of the midday clientele. Here, too, he is known.

'Eh bien, M'sieu Frédéric, ça va, la santé?'

'Très bien, Martial, je vous remercie.'

'Qu'est-ce qu'on vous sert aujourd'hui, M'sieu Frédéric?'

'Un express et un verre d'eau fraiche, s'il vous plaît, Martial.'

For Frederick rarely drinks, and in any case seems to

despise any additional stimulus which might heighten and ultimately falsify his own excellent imagination.

Finally, as the crowd drifts away from the café, Frederick takes his leave of the owner, settles his hat once more on his head, and goes out in search of lunch. He prefers to leave it late, for then he can enjoy the spectacle of the Vieux Port slumbering in the early afternoon heat as he sips his coffee and lights his cigar on the terrace of whatever restaurant he has chosen for that day. Frederick is abstemious, and although no longer mindful of his thickening waistline, prefers to eat a modest meal, perhaps merely a grilled sole or an escalope of veal and a little *salade cuite*, before settling down to his half-hour of contemplation with his coffee and his cigar. Now the sky is powdery white with heat and he can no longer make out the horizon; cars dazzle him with the reflection of the sun on their chrome, and in the longer and longer intervals of quiet, he can hear the creaking of the masts of the little boats in the harbour. Draining his coffee-cup, Frederick asks for the bill, enquires after the health of the lady at the cash desk who nods to him and mimics a reply, and glances to left and right before deciding which route to take to his afternoon place of entertainment. He will either walk along the front, made giddy by the brilliant light and the swoop of traffic, or, more usually, thread his way through the back streets, where trees and rough pavements soon give way to commercial arcades selling the sort of odourless and manufactured produce for which Frederick has no use: magazines, sun glasses, picture postcards, stamps. Once past the Place Masséna, the town is of no further interest to him. He hardly notices it.

At the Ruhl they know him, of course. They are assured that he will spend no more than an hour at the tables, that he will bet modestly, and neither win nor lose a great deal, and that he will be on respectful and easy terms with the ladies who come there, carefully coiffed and made-up, every afternoon, ostensibly to take tea, in fact to attach to themselves a dancing partner, even if they have to pay for one. Frederick is at ease here, and the management are always pleased to see him; his good nature and his good manners ensure that no lady will remain too pathetically and too obviously on her own for more than five or ten minutes. Compliments have always come easily to Frederick; therefore he considers it quite natural to steer these ladies round the tables and to offer them tea. Sometimes the ladies order something stronger and suggest that he stay on for dinner, but Frederick has never cared for that sort of behaviour. In Frederick's universe, the man offers and the woman gratifies. It would seem a reversal of the natural order to proceed in any other way, and indeed he has never needed to do so. Therefore, after a cup of lemon tea and a little expert and desultory conversation, so that the lady should not feel herself to have been offended, he looks around for his panama hat, stands up, and, kissing the lady's hand, takes his leave.

He never stays later than four o'clock. By this time he is feeling a little tired, a little less than the immaculate self which he presented to the world that morning, in the shining air of Bordighera. On the train he pats down a yawn and applies himself to the evening paper which he has bought at the station, noticing with a slight exclamation of distaste that the print has soiled his hands. No matter; at the Hotel Windsor he will ask the upstairs chambermaid Maria to draw his bath as soon as he gets back, and he will recline in the coolish water, scented with New Mown Hay, until he feels his energies return. Then he will dress in his hotelier's evening wear: an immaculate pale cotton suit with matching tie, a fresh shirt, a clean linen handkerchief. He will smooth his sleek greying hair down with his father's silver brushes, which came to him as a matter of course, and, no longer noticing his pear-shaped figure or his dark brown face, he will go downstairs, and, with a discreet but none the less heartfelt kiss, will imply to Evie that she is now free until dinner.

These early evening hours are when Frederick both lays himself out to please and excels himself. Not a guest enters the lobby of the Hotel Windsor after a weary day on the beach or sight-seeing further down the coast but does not feel a lightening of the spirit on encountering Frederick in his pale blue or his pale grey suit, always ready to order a late cup of tea for them and to hear about their day's adventures. Frederick's sybaritic leanings incline him towards indulgence and he has a special smile with which he listens to feminine chatter; it is with a lighter step that so many women guests go up to take their baths and to decide what to wear for the evening. Dinner is a fairly formal affair: Evie and Frederick dine together at a small table slightly out of earshot of the other guests; the children having eaten earlier, either in their suite, if the maids are not too busy, or, more probably, in the kitchen, where they can more easily satisfy their robust appetites. Evie and Frederick have coffee served for all in the salon rather than at the tables, an English habit which makes a favourable impression on the guests, many of whom have returned to the hotel two or three times. When they have enquired after the health of the one or two carefully selected retired couples who intend to spend the winter there, Evie and Frederick tend to say good-night to everyone and to slip out, knowing that they have stimulated the sort of remarks which will be made about them in their absence. 'A quite devoted couple, it seems.' 'Yes, isn't it charming? And they always take this evening walk together before they retire for the night. I find it quite touching.' 'So delightful. It makes for such a pleasant atmosphere.'

149

In the scented night Evie and Frederick take their late walk, arm in arm, sometimes hand in hand. The sky is now an impenetrable indigo, yet along the horizon there is still a faint smudge of salmon-coloured brilliance. The wind rustles the leathery palm leaves and the oranges and lemons glow on the trees as if lit from within. Amber light gushes from the café, where the coffee machine gleams and the scent of vanilla is now mingled with the aroma of cigarettes. Evie and Frederick walk up the steep Corso Italia, away from the sea, away from the station, to the higher ground above the little town. Here, like an elderly couple, they sit on a municipal seat, and here Frederick smokes his second and last cigar of the day. They sit in wordless companionship, looking down on the dark vulture-like shapes of the palm trees, hearing nothing but the whine of a passing moped. Strange, how peaceable Evie has become, she who used to be so noisy and so disruptive. Strange, how excellent this marriage has proved to be, the man offering, the woman gratifying. Strange, how fearless and how original they are away from the constrictions of home and family. Strange, how rooted they appear to be in this frivolous place, divorced from serious need or concern. Soon they will rise to their feet, take each other's hand, and slowly wander back to the Hotel Windsor. They will appreciate the new keenness of the air as a little wind blows up and the houses darken. In their room they will find the bed turned down on both sides, and the shutters closed. Evie will light an incense stick to keep mosquitoes at bay. In no more than a few minutes they will have undressed, kissed, and fallen asleep, safe and calm in the conviction of another beautiful day tomorrow, under the same unalterable sky.

No wonder Frederick never seriously considers going home again.

T W E L V E

Betty spends a lot of time reflecting on the meanness of people, their selfishness, their lack of humanity. 'Lack of humanity' is her rather noble way of putting it; what she really objects to is the fact that she is not having the good time she always promised herself. Sitting beside her swimming pool, in lime-green lounging pyjamas, she ruminates on various grievances in the hot and characterless garden in which she finds herself permanently exiled. To begin with, she never wanted to come to Beverly Hills, which is not at all to her liking. On the boat, a new bride, she had been deliriously happy. Not only had she married a handsome young husband, but the first days of her married life had passed in an endless and intoxicating whirl of cocktails, dances, fancy-dress parties, keep-fit classes and deck games which made of life a prolongation of that childhood she had been so anxious to shed. It seemed to her then, in the slight atmosphere of hysteria engendered by the panic from which they were all escaping, that if life could go on like this she would never grumble again. Her eyes like dark glass after so many cocktails, so many late nights, her hair blown into a halo by the strong Atlantic air, her bangles slipping up and down her thin arms, her flimsy chiffon blouses – in peach, in coffee, in lilac – tossed carelessly all over the cabin, Betty, in the early days of her marriage, revealed an inventiveness, a love of pleasure, which finally subjugated the obdurate Max who became temporarily enslaved by his wife. What Betty did not know was that Max, who was rather like his uncle in this respect, particularly savoured that wild unstudied side of her nature that could turn, with equally keen appetite, from simple physical greed to the stern and unforgiving appraisal of her appearance before some evening party, when, at her dressing-table, she would moisten her lips, narrow her eyes, take up her mirror and study her reflection from every angle. When she was obsessed with herself in this way Betty would brush Max aside as if he had suddenly become unimportant, as indeed he had, for Betty's concentration on her desires, her looks, her performance, was unvarying. Both uncle and nephew would delight in ordering some dish for her and watching her, as, dainty as a cat, she would eat her way through it, deaf and blind to what was being said or done in her presence. At moments like these Max would congratulate himself on having snared an original, a little animal who would keep him amused for as long as any woman had ever kept him amused, which was not very long, but, in his view, long enough.

Betty, of course, was building herself up for her future, for her great career on the screen. To this end, she practised those emotions which she did not feel. So that, in between the bouts of frenetic dancing and the late nights and the dressing up, all of which came entirely naturally, Betty would languish and sigh and flirt with anyone who came near. None of this troubled Max, who knew exactly what was going on, but it got her rather a bad name as far as the other passengers were concerned. Betty put this down to sheer jealousy on the part of women whose husbands had become assiduous in their attention to her; little did those husbands know that it was in the interests

of making an entrance that Betty would stroll languor-
ously on to the first-class deck at eleven every morning,
and, twisting her key in her hand, would enquire, with
the slightest hint of a lisp, 'Now which of you kind
gentlemen is going to find me a nice chair? I feel really
lazy today.' And, the chair having been found, she would
stretch out, purr like a cat, and hitch up her white linen
skirt, revealing her firmly muscled little legs and her
dancer's feet in tiny white shoes. This was all that she
intended. Having made her entrance, she was quite content to let the whole thing lapse until it was time to make
another. But various men in blazers were apt to hover
around, distracting her and annoying their wives. 'It's
nothing to do with me,' Betty would say, opening her
eyes wide, when Mr Markus hinted that she should be
more discreet. 'I can't help it if they all want to be with
me. I didn't ask them to sit with me, did I?' And she
would have no hesitation in blaming the women, whom
she would describe as mean and selfish, the terms that she
would later apply to all those who cast a shadow on her
progress through life.

New York, predictably, enchanted her. She was so
gloriously, so outrageously happy when Mr Markus took
her for her first walk down Madison Avenue that he was
genuinely touched, and, seeing her clasp the collar of her
poor little fur jacket to her throat in unthinking rapture, he
abandoned his usual mood of fairly gloomy impassivity,
took her into a shop, and bought her a proper fur coat.
That was probably her happiest time. When Mr Markus
took her into Central Park, thinking to amuse her with
the zoo and the children, she tugged at his arm, turned
her face pleadingly upward, and begged, 'Couldn't we
just look at the shops?' When Mr Markus and Max were
busy seeing people in the film world, all of whom seemed
to Betty to be as gloomy as Mr Markus himself, she

would cheerfully go out alone, and in the crystal light of late autumn, would promenade deliciously up and down Madison Avenue, Park Avenue, or (her favourite) Fifth Avenue, as if there were no more to New York than those three beautiful streets, and as if she had been destined to wear a fine fur coat and idle her days away, buying perhaps a bottle of scent or a pair of gloves or wondering where to get her hair done. Money seemed to be fairly easily available, and Betty spent lavishly. One day, she thought, she must send a little present home to her mother, and possibly her sister. But they had such boringly correct taste that Betty really wondered if they would appreciate what New York had to offer. She would take a look through the big department stores, to see if there were anything plain enough to suit them. She would do that any day now. But in the meantime, that white silk kimono with the pattern of black feathers scattered all over it, that would go beautifully with her own more forceful looks.

Had they been able to stay in New York, Betty might conceivably have gone on being happy. When it became clear that in order to find work Mr Markus and Max would have to move to California, Betty even suggested that they go on ahead, leaving her in New York to await their return. She did not understand that the film industry required their constant presence, particularly as they were so dependent on their contacts and so anxious to work hard. 'But I shan't be able to wear my coat there,' she objected. The delights of Hollywood were briefly described to her, and then, because she was now a Hungarian wife, and no longer allowed to be superior in temperament to her husband, who might just be a genius, she was told to pack her bags and face up to the fact that she must either make friends with the other women in the film colony or be prepared to spend a great deal of time on her own.

She did not make many friends. All the women she knew were adorable to begin with but were apt to turn mean and selfish within a very short space of time. Betty enjoyed a quarrel, but she also enjoyed having the last word, a predilection which she shared with many of the Hollywood wives who, like herself, had little to do with their days. Betty would put down the telephone triumphantly on one of these former friends, only to realize that she had forgotten to ask the name of that new hairdresser that everyone was raving about, and be forced to call back. In this way she had many acquaintances, very few of whom she trusted or who trusted her, and need never lack for company if only she would condescend to ask for it. But her constant stories about these acquaintances, and the grudges she seemed to build up so easily, became wearisome to listen to, and she began to bore her husband.

She bought clothes, dozens of them, in the light bright colours that she favoured, and she would change several times a day. Max usually brought someone home in the evening, so there was a reason to have a long scented bath at about five o'clock and get into something dramatic and floating, but after she had taken all that trouble it was too unkind of them to talk business as if she were simply not there. When Max required her to give a dinner party she came out of it rather splendidly, for most of the male guests adored her English accent and her piquant looks, and if there were enough people she need not bother with the women at all. The women, in any event, could take good care of themselves. When she idled away an afternoon with any of these women, either beside her own pool or somebody else's, she heard talk of money, of infidelity, of settlements. This bewildered her, and she was still enough of her mother's daughter to consider it very *mauvais genre*. After one of these afternoons, she would treat her husband with more care and respect, would be quiet when he wanted to be quiet, and would place a little dish of sweetmeats at his elbow as he worked. All in all, Betty was a good wife. And Max, although occasionally unfaithful, had the good taste to ensure that she never learned of it. Location trips, he explained. Reno. Las Vegas. You wouldn't enjoy it. All that sand.

One of the mean and selfish things that people do to Betty is not to send her money from England. It seems to her to be lacking in humanity that Alfred, who is, as everybody knows, a rich man, does not make her an allowance. She does not need the money, of course, but she is on the lookout for injustice. Therefore she writes to Alfred, putting in a bid for her share of 'my father's money'. He has become, in retrospect, her father and nobody else's. She is so used to thinking of herself that her brothers and her sister have no reality for her. They exist in her memory, and she is incurious about their present life. In fact they serve only to fuel those anecdotes about her childhood with which she regales her friends or Max's colleagues or, if there is nobody else immediately available, her maid or the man who comes to clean the pool. When performing this particular number at dinner parties Betty's eyes widen and her face takes on the look of the spoilt child she has grown into. These anecdotes make an initial impact but generally fall on deaf ears. Childhood is not much valued here in Hollywood. And with so many exiles and refugees in their circle, it is not always entirely tactful to refer to her uneventful early years in such sentimental terms. 'You never talked about your childhood when we met in Paris,' Max says to her curiously one evening, as they are undressing for bed. 'Why go into it now? You are getting older, not younger.' At which she flounces into the bathroom and does not speak to him until the following day.

She never made a film, of course. The early rising, the harsh lights, the heavy make-up, would not have suited her. In any event she was never really given the choice. Mr Markus fixed up a screen test for her but oddly enough, or perhaps not, she came across as impossibly mannered, and her sultry expression merely made her look bad-tempered. Conferring with Max, Mr Markus tried to salvage Betty's honour by offering her a very small part ('A cameo,' they explained to her) as a waitress in a French *estaminet* frequented by international criminals. She refused it with a certain amount of shouting and screaming and it took several days to calm her down. She had expected the lead, and to this day blames the meanness and selfishness of the director who, she is convinced, wanted the part for his mistress. She still refers to this incident with some acrimony although it took place a very long time ago. Since then she has formed the habit of reading novels and proposing themes to Max on the basis of what she has read. Betty is the only member of the family to whom reading does not present itself as a silent activity. These scenarios would involve huge budgets, expensive adaptations, and of course a prominent part for Betty. 'I see myself as Madeleine,' she says to Max as they eat dinner. (Or Dolores. Or Andrea.) 'I could really bring something to a part like that. And perhaps they could work in a dance routine. A ballroom scene. Or you could do it in costume.' Max knows how to deal with all this. 'I am at the mercy of the finance department,' he says. What really annoys him is her insistence on telling him the plot of anything she happens to be reading, which makes for some very dull evenings.

Max, in any event, is working in different directions, a fact which Betty manages to overlook. Max is doing very well. He was one of the first to respond to the possibilities of television and an audience so captive that it does not have to stir from its favourite chair. Within the restrictive boundaries of the small black and white screen Max is a perceptive and a creative cineaste. He specializes in police dramas, with the sympathy very clearly bestowed on the outlaw, the fugitive, the man on the run. This format has the added advantage of permitting any number of settings. Max has had men on the run in sunlit Paris, in foggy London, in rainy New York. What he is good at is not the thrill of the chase, or the escape, which is entirely predictable, but the life of the streets in which the outlaw or fugitive spends much of his time trying to assume a new identity. No doubt Max has a personal feeling for such a predicament, although he would laugh at the suggestion, not being a man who cares to share that part of his life with anyone. In this he is unlike Betty who can summon up instant rapture or instant despair when referring to an incident in her own past. Some of Max's most haunting images come from a certain area of his carefully stored memory bank. Thus the American public has come to know and to appreciate that shot of the concierge with her cat, or the little boy carrying home the long stick of bread, or the cobbles of a street in Montmartre glistening faintly after a summer shower. Max's films are interesting because they concentrate on emptiness, on the time before things happen, the time when the outlaw might just get away with it. He also has a deep nostalgia for the world and the time he left behind. His men tend to wear rather long leather coats, his women fox furs and little tilted hats. Max is making quite a name for himself. As time goes on it could be said that he lives for his work.

Betty did not expect to be left alone quite so much. This is another grievance to be added to the rapidly mounting pile. 'I'm sure you could find a place for me at the studios,' she tells Max. 'I'm very sympathetic and I know how artists behave.' Or, 'I really ought to have a seat on the board. After all, I've been in show business myself. I know all about it.' Max is quite capable of dealing with this. In his experience all wives are discontented and can be placated with gifts of jewellery. And Betty, who is now voluptuously plump, is still a very attractive woman. Although permanently complaining about something or other, she has acquired sultry clinging ways which sustain his interest in her. She is one of those naturally unfair women who rule by bouts of ill-humour and whose sudden unpredictable changes of mood bring about relief, gratitude, and a general lightening of the atmosphere. Max is used to dealing with women and their changing moods, and indeed would not know what to do with the sort of wife who tries to please. If he had a wife like that, a wife who waited on him, laundered his shirts and scented them with lavender and vetiver, cooked him his favourite dishes, and enquired sympathetically whether he had had a hard day, he would be far more unfaithful than he actually is. Max requires diversion and contention from a woman, and either by luck or by judgment Betty supplies him with both.

The one thing Betty has never been able to recapture is that sense of effortless superiority that she possessed at the age of sixteen. Where once she had only to display herself against the dreamy passivity of her sister Mimi, she is now surrounded by women of her own type, all of them, according to Betty, 'lacking in humanity'. For this reason her thoughts sometimes go back to Mimi, especially when she receives the really surprising news of her sister's marriage. Betty has no clear memory of Lautner, to whom she never paid any attention, but she is quite glad that Mimi did not marry Frank, with whom she has completely lost touch, not having bothered to inform him that she was leaving Paris. Mimi married!

That only leaves Alfred, with whom Betty has never been on good terms. She must look for a lovely wedding present from Max and herself. She really must make time to do this, perhaps tomorrow. But when the wedding photographs arrive and she sees how astonishingly prosperous Mimi looks in her white dress and with all those flowers, Betty turns thoughtful. She reflects that Mimi seems to be doing very well for herself. She then remembers that her family made no contribution towards the cost of her own wedding, which in fact cost absolutely nothing, and from the pile of discarded dresses which she had put on one side for the maid, she retrieves an orange chiffon evening gown and a short brocade jacket, parcels them up, and sends them off with a card in her extravagant hand: 'Love and kisses, Betty'. After all, the dress, when Max bought it for her, had been very expensive, and she has only worn it two or three times.

The more Betty thinks about it, the more this wedding inflames her with a sense of injustice. She particularly dislikes the way Max pores keenly over the photographs, and, pointing with his long forefinger, demands, 'And this one? Who is this? Whose mistress is this Dolly? She is very fine, but the other one, the little one, is more *sympathique*.' Betty snatches the photograph from him. 'Nettie?' she asks doubtfully. 'Well, she was pretty as a child, but I don't think she's very remarkable now. And that awful hat.' She continues to study the photographs, in odd moments, as does Max. Quite frequently, each will come upon the other, looking at this family group. Max seems fascinated by the array of handsome women, by the supporting cast of good-natured men. It is like a dream of home to him. Betty merely notices, with some annoyance, how everyone seems to have grown up, grown into a state of possession, while she has been absent, in this rented house, beside a chemically coloured pool, on someone else's land, in a distant country. And they all look so rich! How could her Mama not have sent her the money to attend this wedding, where she could have made a spectacular entrance and stunned everyone with her transatlantic sophistication? She forgets that she has not yet replied to the letter informing her of Mimi's forthcoming marriage, a letter to which Sofka has added, in her angular but now shaky handwriting, 'We should so love to see you, my darling.' Ignoring this, Betty considers it outrageous that Alfred, with all his money, should not have sent two first-class tickets and arranged a welcome. The prodigal returns! Betty forgets that she has enough money, or rather enough of Max's money, to arrange her own passage home, that she could, on receipt of Mimi's letter, on an impulse, have bought an airline ticket and gone home to embrace her mother. But that is not the way in which Betty thinks it should have been arranged. Her family should have petitioned her, begged her, postponed the wedding until she should have imparted her plans, waited, with mounting anxiety, to see whether or not she would be able to attend. And the least they could have done would be to have invited Max, whom they have never met. This is Alfred's doing, of course. Alfred was always down on her.

Mama is getting old, thinks Betty, with a tiny thrill of fear. And when she is no longer there, whose favourite will I be?

Suddenly the sun in this place looks garish and the scenery insipid. Max's images on the television screen seem to reflect a denser reality than that enjoyed by Betty in her high-heeled sandals and her lounging pyjamas. Her mind slips gratefully into those dark, cool, bluish streets, those gas-lit alleys, that provincial café, that park at midnight with its dripping trees where the man on the run waits for the woman who has sworn that she will go with him. Betty watches, achingly, as the figure in the long leather coat, with his hat pulled well down, slouches, unrecognized, through a curiously empty Pigalle. Max is flattered by this new interest she shows in his work. But Betty only really sees herself, tapping her way confidently to the stage door of the Moulin Rouge on the day of her first (and only) audition. She feels, with all the pain of true nostalgia, the crispness of the November air in Paris, smells the coffee and the cigarettes, settles her hand more firmly round the handle of her little make-up case. She remembers dancing with aplomb and attack; she remembers how little she thought of her gift, sleeping late in those lazy mornings, buying herself cakes to eat as a treat on her way home, gradually taking less exercise, putting on weight. Now she would no longer dare to try on her practice dress. Now she prefers loose filmy clothes, although her legs are still good.

Max, grunting slightly, switches off the television, stubs out his cigarette, and sits with a cautious hand to his chest. Indigestion or something else frequently finds him in this position. Betty at such moments makes him a cup of tea and reminds him that they have arranged to meet some people downtown for dinner and that when he has drunk his tea he had better take a shower and change. Fortunately Betty is not one of those wives who make a fuss. It would not occur to her to call a doctor, and in this way Max is preserved from an invalid's regimen, but will continue to lead his intense and sceptical and by this stage very withdrawn existence. He is grateful to his wife for not noticing that anything is amiss, grateful too that she is tough enough to take whatever may come, grateful that their love is not of the overwhelming variety that makes such thoughts unbearable.

When Betty finds Max sitting on the bed, staring yet again at the wedding photographs, she tells him quite sharply that if he does not stop mooning about in this uncharacteristic way they will soon be late. When he says that he does not feel like going out she reproaches him for being selfish. When, with a sigh, he gets up, having weighed in the balance the very few options open to him, Betty exclaims, 'And about time too!' When he slowly topples forward Betty is at her dressing-table, trying on and discarding various pairs of earrings. In that way, when she looks in the mirror, she sees behind her reflection only absence.

In the days of terror that follow Betty refuses to leave Max's hospital bed. There is no need, they tell her, for her to stay. He will pull through: it was not a serious attack. But she sits there, her eyes wide, her hair uncombed, clutching his hand. The room is full of stupendous flowers and unreal-looking fruit. Mr Markus comes every day and so do many of Betty's friends, those friends whom she has always rather disliked. She is anxious for them all to leave, and despite their sudden kindness and the disquiet in their eyes she hastens them to the door. She knows, without being told, that Max will recover but that he will be diminished, and she is unwilling for anyone to share this knowledge. For this reason she sits by him, holding his hand, letting him sleep, urging him silently to come back to her, promising, in her mind, that she will be good.

They are a quiet couple now. Max cannot work much, and he has become rather morose. The illness has affected him more slowly but more profoundly. Betty looks after him with great devotion. Thanks to Alfred, to whom Betty wrote as soon as Max came home, they live quite comfortably. Of course, life is very dull. Sometimes Betty wonders if she will ever have anyone to talk to again. In the afternoons, when Max is having his rest, she wanders down to the pool. She stares at the water. 'Isn't it a pretty colour?' she says forlornly to the man who has come to filter it. 'I had a hair ribbon just that shade when I was a little girl.'

THIRTEEN

BEFORE ENTERING the bedroom Mimi composes her face. She takes a deep breath, straightens her back, and opens the door. 'Look, Mama,' she says. 'Dolly and Hal have sent these lovely flowers.' She puts the heavy vase down on a little table where Sofka can see it from the bed. Sofka's eyes never leave Mimi's face. My poor girl, she thinks. You are beginning to treat me as if I were your child. Then it must be nearly over with me.

Mimi tiptoes from the room, closing the door quietly behind her. Since that bout of influenza, from which Sofka does not appear to recover, the drawing-room at Bryanston Square is rarely empty. Mimi is there every day, of course, and Lautner joins her devotedly whenever he can. Alfred stays in every evening now. Sometimes Dolly and Hal come round, sometimes Nettie and Will, sometimes all four of them. On occasions like these, smiles grow wistful, conversation more poignant. In the kitchen the girls, Lili and Ursie, are kept busy making relays of tea and coffee, cutting up cheese-cake, honey cake, almond cake. Sometimes the atmosphere is quite animated. They pull the curtains, switch on all the lamps, bustle around with plates and trays, go through to the kitchen to see if the girls are all right, take it in turns to sit with Sofka, come back to report no change, stand up again and produce cigars, offer brandy. This atmosphere is very persuasive, almost festive. Only Lautner looks uneasy. Eventually he waylays Alfred, who has continued to dislike him. 'Should you send for Frederick?' he asks. Alfred dislikes him even more. 'There is no need,' he replies. 'My mother is a little tired, no more than that. As you can see, she is being looked after perfectly well. Are you coming back inside?' he asks rudely, indicating the door of the drawing-room. 'Or are you taking Mimi home? She looks dreadful, by the way. Are you sure *she* is being properly looked after?' And with that he turns his back and prepares to rejoin the others. He will never forgive Lautner for making Mimi pregnant.

Sofka is aware of all this and at the same time profoundly indifferent. She knows that Frederick would not come even if they sent for him, as she senses they might. She knows, but cannot be bothered to tell them, that Frederick, without any of his motives being clear to him, would simply prolong all discussion of such a visit until the reason for it faded from his mind. He is like that; he delays until action becomes irrelevant. Sofka can see him smiting his forehead in amazement, as he used to do when he was a young man. 'But why didn't you tell me?' he will say. 'I would have come at once.' Useless to explain to him that the others are so fearful that they might not make their news entirely clear, that Sofka's illness or weakness or fatigue, whatever it is, has been veiled in so many euphemisms that even if the message were sent Frederick might have some excuse for not finding it terribly urgent. By this time only Sofka is capable of stating, 'I long for you. Let me see you once before I die.' And she is too tired even to frame the thought and its consequences. But as she lies there, raised on many pillows in her soft white bed, it is of Frederick and of Betty that she thinks. She sees them quite accurately: bathed in sunshine, in clothes that are not quite serious, exiles, no longer young. They are her favourites, now as then. For Mimi and for Alfred she has only tenderness, respect, acknowledgment. She knows that they will be there to the end. But, in death as in life, it is the absent one who sees to it that the business will remain unfinished, the farewells unsaid: it is the prodigal who does not return who makes the idea of goodness a mockery. Sofka, indifferent on her pillows, feels a throb of sadness only for those who are not gathered in the adjoining room.

The one whose presence she finds easiest is Lautner, whose devotion is so simple, so absolute, and yet so weightless that there is no need to apologize to him or to reassure him or to thank him. At the very beginning of this illness, she whispered to Lautner, 'Look after Mimi,' and since then has said nothing. She saw his eyes fill with tears; she felt his lips brush her hand. Now it is easier not to talk. Strange how Lautner is a better nurse than the nurse herself. When Lautner enters Sofka's bedroom and sits down by the bed, the nurse retires quietly to the kitchen for a cup of tea. Lautner notices little things that the nurse misses. The fine linen handkerchief has been creased; he will put a fresh one into the hand that lies inert on the lace counterpane. He will sprinkle a little mimosa scent on the lamp, to make the room smell of spring. He will touch Sofka's lips with glycerine and rosewater, so that they do not become too dry. And although she no longer responds, he will tell her in pleasant detail of the weather outside, describe for her the position of Dorn and Co. on the stock-market, sometimes read her an item from the newspaper: the weather in Nice, in Los Angeles. She likes to see him sitting there, with his newspaper. She likes this reminder of the masculine world, so authoritative, so reassuring, so unlike the tempestuous and secret comings and goings of Alfred. Lautner calls her 'Mama', which Alfred despises. Alfred sees it as an attempt to curry favour. But Sofka and Lautner know that it is the word that Lautner has been longing to use for all his adult life. If it means little to Sofka now, it means all the world to Lautner. It means coming home.

Lautner gets up and draws the curtains, patting their heavy folds carefully together. 'Strange, how early it gets dark now,' he says to Sofka, resuming his seat by the bed. 'As we left home I said to Mimi, "I will leave some lights on, darling. It will make it more cheerful when we come back." Because I like to keep her spirits up, you know. She is so imaginative, Mama. And with the baby coming, she needs to be kept calm. But she is quite well, quite well. You can see for yourself. Perfectly well. I make sure that she eats properly, and gets her rest. And it is good for her to see her family in the evenings, like this. That way the change does not seem too great to her. It is a miracle, of course.' He looks down at his hands, smooths the newspaper, composes himself. 'Clear and sunny in Nice,' he says. 'Fine and warm.'

He is a good man, thinks Sofka. He is like my father. Strange how he calls me Mama. Was he here at the beginning? I came to this country as a girl, leaving my parents behind me. I never saw them again. I married and I left home, but none of us cried. My parents were happy for me, and they had my sisters. I was very proud. My husband was so handsome, so attractive to women. Yet he chose me. I never regretted it, never minded his flirtations. His death was sudden, peaceful. I was spared the sight of him changing into a fretful old man. And as I remember him he was the gallant suitor he had always been. I had the children then, of course. That was what he wanted, it seemed. The wife and children at home, the ladies outside. But I didn't mind. For when I had the children they were more important to me than anything in the world. Little Alfred, trying so hard to please me. The girls in the old nursery. Mimi's lovely hair. My beautiful life.

Lautner thinks, they should have sent for Frederick. It will not be long now. Mimi thinks, if it is a girl I shall call her Sophie. Mama would like that. Alfred thinks, they are all making a fuss. Typical. As soon as she is a little better I shall take her down to the country. Fresh air is what she needs. It was always too stuffy in this flat. Dolly thinks, when will he leave his mother alone and come to me? Is the moment getting any nearer? If it is not, I will wait no longer. Nettie thinks, poor Tanti. I never saw enough of her, never felt entitled to come back, bore them all a grudge for sending me away all that long time ago. Strange to be back. Strange to see Alfred again, to be one of them again. Just like old times.

Truth to tell, the atmosphere in that drawing-room is not unlike one of those weddings at which the whole clan foregathered. As the girls, Lili and Ursie, come in with silver trays of tea and honey cake, Nettie and Dolly fuss around Mimi who smiles, blushes, much as she always has done. She is thinner, of course, and the bulk of her pregnancy paradoxically makes her look rather gaunt but otherwise she has not changed much. Perhaps the features are more definite, the movements more confident; perhaps she has lost that faltering walk she used to have, perhaps she has lost that enquiring hopeful smile. One would hope so, for she is nearly forty. But generally speaking, the men of this family age more quickly than the women. Hal looks quite dry, quite exhausted, while Dolly is more effulgent than ever. She has done her hair a new way, winding it in a mass behind her head, and even for this simple visit she is wearing a black lace dress. Nettie thinks that dress is in frightful taste. Just like Dolly to usurp the mourning function as well as presuming to treat the evening as a normal evening party. Nettie feels all sorts of sadness. She, like Alfred, was rushed too soon away from her childhood, never had time to be young, was instructed to be an adult before she was ready. When she came back from finishing school, her mother had a husband almost lined up for her: Will, with whom, on the whole, she has been happy. But no children. Strange, how both Dolly and she have had no children, and inexplicable, unless you believe in those old superstitions about the wrong partner producing no children. She has not been unhappy, thinks Nettie, but Dolly is beginning to look hard, cruel. Hal sees it all, of course. For a long time now Nettie has disguised from herself the entanglement which is now obvious; it has kept her away from her aunt's house. Tact, perhaps, or distaste. In any event, a desire not to see, not to witness. All that is over, or should be. It is a long time now since she and Alfred danced at that wedding, when they were children. She used to think of him, learning to be a man while she sent him postcards of the lake at sunset. She thought he might be waiting for her when she came back. But Dolly had been going out with Frederick, and both girls were eager to be married, and so they had married. And it is only childhood sentiment that turns her mind back to those remote days, because childhood, Nettie knows, is so easily lost, and perhaps she may be forgiven for clinging to these very distant memories.

Dolly, with one white hand, fingers her pearls, and then lets the hand rest on her black lace breast, holding it there, fingers outspread, until Alfred obeys her will and turns his eyes to her. Oblivious of the others she keeps his eyes captive, appropriating him from this family gathering, extricating him from all other loyalties, claiming him. Dolly is fearless. She will have this man, whom the old woman in the bedroom would deny her: the dead have no power against the living, however binding their wishes may once have been. Hal thinks, drily, the moment is approaching. Will thinks the same.

Alfred, confused between the claims of past and present, rejects both. He refuses to believe that anything has changed. Or does he? Alfred, in fact, begins to resemble a character in classical tragedy or allegorical painting: on the one hand a figure embodying loyalty, piety, constraint, and on the other the irresistible lineaments of subversion. To do what Alfred is almost about to do requires nerve and practice: Alfred has acquired a little nerve but perhaps not enough practice. But Alfred is aware of the urge to do something. As far as he is concerned his life has been spent in the wings while other members of his family have arranged their futures to suit themselves. The defection, as he sees it, of Frederick and Betty has left him with the fate of Mimi and his mother entirely on his hands. And now that Mimi, apparently the weakest link, in truth the most beloved, has mocked him by this ludicrous marriage to Lautner, leaving him with a mother who gives every sign of declining into gentle invalidism, Alfred sees no need to sacrifice himself further. Since Mimi has made a mockery of Alfred's dependability by behaving as a woman of ordinary strength, and seems determined to pursue her familial functions along divergent lines, Alfred will have no more of it. If Lautner appears to be so devoted a son-in-law as almost to have usurped the position of a son, then let him make himself useful. If Lautner refuses to remain marginal, then let him be central. Let him assume his major-domo functions here instead of in Kentish Town, and thus release Alfred for that life of risk and impropriety which has been his temptation, his fantasy, and his promised reward ever since he discovered, to his infinite regret and relief, that the farther shores of the real world were not within his compass. How long ago it now seems that he sat at his father's desk, reading *The Conquest of Peru*, with Nettie's postcard of Lac Léman by his side!

Although as discreet, handsome, and taciturn in appearance as he always had it in him to become, Alfred, inwardly, now begins to develop towards a state bordering on psychopathy. He begins to envisage his actions as being entirely without consequences. He will, he thinks, take Dolly away from Hal; he will simply run off with her, leaving the rest of them to rearrange themselves as well as they can. He will do this not necessarily because this is what he wants but because he has never had his own way, and because his exacerbated manhood demands, now, imperatively, that he have his own way in as spectacular a manner as possible, as if to atone for all the good behaviour that has been expected of him in the past. He has, in all conscience, paid his dues to society and to his family. Above all, to his family. Now it seems to him that he must vindicate his buried self, that essential self still burning beneath the lava accretions of duty, foresight, prudence, accountability, reputation, regularity, good manners, and the unvarying performance of the high-principled man of affairs. As he sees it, the time has come for him to give others cause for comment. He would almost like to force them into a state of alarm, of speculation, of disarray: he would like to be a renegade, like Frederick, like Betty, safe and untouched in their sunlit exile, while he, here, in this dark curtained room, remains monstrously virtuous, his mother's son. Alfred, longing for the day when, obeying some internal signal shown only to himself, he will make good his escape, is actively biding his time. One day, quite simply, he will shed his habits, like the sober and immaculate suits he always wears; he will walk out of the door and start his life again, somewhere else, with Dolly as the enabling factor. In gardenia-scented exile, he will force them all to take note.

Alfred almost sees that, when the time comes for him to release his internal imperatives once again, he will abandon Dolly to her fate. He almost sees, and in this he is percipient, that Dolly is not a long-term prospect. Dolly is danger, risk, precipitancy; Dolly is a pretext. With Dolly he will open Pandora's box, letting loose confusion into the world, into his world. But when the demons of confusion have escaped from Pandora's box, and only Hope remains, then, Alfred knows (but represses the knowledge as being untimely) that Dolly will not quite do. Dolly's high-risk factor, compounded as it is of her beauty and her gift for appropriation, will dictate her next move. No doubt Hal will take her back. If not Hal, someone else. Here Alfred, once again, comes seriously close to that abnormal state in which he attributes motives of carelessness and attributes of safety to those whom he should know better. Hal may indeed take Dolly back, but, by the same token, he may not necessarily let her go in the first place.

Dolly, idle white hand on black lace breast, watches, lazy-eyed, as her tardy lover wills himself into a state of action. Hal's eyes are lowered impassively as, apparently without volition, he twists his wedding-ring on his finger. Nettie's eyes are wide with sorrow as she follows Lautner's progress in and out of the room. It is left to Will, good-natured and always mildly effervescent, to sustain the conversation, which he does, teasing Mimi gently and asking her what the baby is to be called. Mimi, in fact, is conscious of nothing but her husband, her baby, and the knowledge that her health has never been better. She sinks unreflecting into the pleasure of these evenings in her old home, with her family around her. As Will keeps up his flow of jokes it is almost possible to forget

173

why they are all gathered here together, evening after evening, in the warm cigar-scented room.

A ring at the doorbell alerts them vaguely that someone has called, but conversation from the kitchen leads them to suppose that it is a visitor for Lili or Ursie. It is known that Lili has a suitor, a noisy and impudent charmer called Benjie. Benjie is something of a playboy and he can afford to be: his father is a dealer in antique furniture, a man of some repute in the trade, and Benjie is supposed to be working for him. All he does at the moment is take Lili off in his car to country auctions: Lili has returned from many an expedition of this kind, starry-eyed, to tell Sofka all about it, and Sofka has promised that when Lili gets married she will have as fine a wedding as if she had been one of Sofka's own daughters. But when the door of the drawing-room opens it reveals not Benjie but Mrs Beck, correct in her decent black coat, her face very faintly and discreetly powdered. 'Why, Mrs Beck,' says Mimi, rising. 'How very nice of you to call.' Mrs Beck takes Mimi's hand and nods to the group. As her eyes come to rest on Dolly they turn pitiless, as they did in the old days of hardship. 'I have come to pay my respects,' says Mrs Beck, accepting a seat. 'I have come to pay my respects to my dear friend Mrs Dorn.'

There is a tiny silence after this remark, as if they have been led back, rather unwillingly, to the reason for their all being here. When the conversation resumes it is of a different order. 'You are well, Mimi, my dear?' Mrs Beck enquires, accepting a cup of tea and a slice of almond cake. 'Very well, thank you, Mrs Beck,' says Mimi, and, to fill the silence, 'Ursie, make fresh tea, will you? And come and join us. Tell Lili and Benjie to come too. Let us all be together.'

So the room fills up, and the very slight ripple caused by Mrs Beck's entrance dies down. Benjie accepts one of

Will's cigars and amuses them with some of his stories about skulduggery in the antique trade. He is a very good raconteur, and even Hal gives a dry laugh. Alfred smiles too, prepared to tolerate them all in the knowledge that he will soon do so no longer. He feels no animosity, is prepared to be large, hospitable, until such time as he decrees that they must get along without him. He is still the householder, the proprietor, the patron. They will lack for nothing, he promises them silently. They may continue as they are. There will be no change, but one day, quite simply, he will no longer be there.

'And how is your mother this evening, Alfred?' asks Mrs Beck, impenitent. 'She is sleeping, Mrs Beck,' Alfred replies. 'I will tell her that you called.' He has always faintly disliked Mrs Beck, with her minatory air, her presence as disturbing as that of an over-active conscience, and in order to compensate for this dislike has provided for her most generously and has taken her son into the firm. This, if he could be bothered to think about it, could amount to yet another instance of good behaviour against which his ultimate villainy must be measured. Alfred, living his temporary fiction of immunity from the rules, consigns Mrs Beck along with the rest of them. No complaints, he trusts? It would appear, as he looks around the room, that there are no complaints.

As the clock in the hall gives its mellow boom Mimi looks up, startled. 'Why,' she says, 'I had no idea it was so late. Joseph, we should be going.' And she gets up heavily, shaking her dress and smoothing it down. It is a general signal. Nettie begins to gather the plates and cups together. 'Leave that, Nettie,' says Dolly sharply. 'The girls will see to it.' Hal purses his lips. Already she has taken command, he thinks. Nettie takes no notice, receives Mrs Beck's cup with a smile. As Mimi is helped into her fur coat by Will she turns to Lautner and asks,

'Should we disturb her?' 'I think not,' he replies. 'She will be sleeping by now.' But he slips out of the room to make sure. Goodbyes are said, lingering and comfortable goodbyes. They will in any event meet again here on the following evening. Benjie kisses Lili's hair and slaps her gently on the bottom. The girls take this opportunity to make their farewells to the company; they will wash up and go to bed if nothing else is needed, they say. 'Nothing else,' smiles Mimi, and she kisses them both good-night, as she has always done. They return her kisses warmly. The girls are no longer afraid of Mimi.

When Lautner returns he says nothing. This is a supremely painful moment for him. His past, his incredible present, inhabit him to the exclusion of all those assembled, of that family with whom he has only honorary kinship, like a temporary visa. Mimi looks up, bright-faced, a little sleepy now. How innocent she is still! Lautner finds that he cannot meet her eyes. 'Sleeping?' she asks, her smile now a little anxious. Lautner knows that he must arrest the general movement away from this warm safe room, but he finds himself incapable of resolving how to bring this about. 'Joseph?' repeats Mimi. Lautner walks slowly over to a small table, stands with his back to them, head bent. He appears to be straightening something on this table, closing the lid of the cigar box. When he turns to face them, they see that he is in fact an old man. 'Oh, Joseph,' whispers Mimi, suddenly not daring to raise her voice. 'Do you think we should send for Frederick?' 'No,' says Lautner. 'There is no need now.'

Immediately Lili and Ursie, alerted by some ancient knowledge, set up a high-pitched keening. This noise becomes wilder, louder, as Mrs Beck, her lips working, takes them into her arms. Benjie, his face red, his hands hanging helplessly at his side, watches them, until, at a

sign from Mrs Beck, he shepherds them both from the
room. 'Tanti,' sighs Nettie, and turns away. Dolly and
Hal stand stock still; after a while Hal puts a hand over
his eyes. Will shakes his head, his cheerful face crumpling.
'Mama?' whispers Mimi fearfully. 'Mama?' Then,
louder, 'Mama? Mama? Mama?' Lautner moves forward,
but he appears not to be in full control of his movements,
and before he can reach her, Mimi has fainted into Nettie's
loving arms.

Alfred has turned to stone. Around him the room is in
confusion. From the kitchen come the sobs and cries of
the girls, now out of control. Those cries will continue
all night as the girls, broken, relive their history, their
earlier losses. Mrs Beck takes Benjie on one side; her task
is to instruct him. He smiles unhappily as she retains him
by the door. Dolly and Hal, after whispered consultation,
turn to go; Dolly makes as if to take Alfred in her arms
but Hal puts a hand on her shoulder to constrain her.
Nettie and Will remain. Lautner has led Mimi to her old
room and sits beside the bed on which she lies, her eyes
closed, her hand pressed to her side. Alfred, staring into
the abyss, walks stiffly to the door and shuts it behind
him.

Obeying some ancestral impulse, Alfred takes a silk
shawl and covers his mother's looking-glass. Then he
turns and takes up his position at the foot of her bed,
where he will remain all night. He is aware of Lautner
coming and going but he will have none of him. In the
intervals of lucidity he hears Lautner speaking quietly on
the telephone; he is dimly grateful to the man for making
those arrangements which must be made. He also hears
the broken cries of the girls, as, turning in their haunted
sleep, they greet their banished ghosts. At some point he
is aware of Lautner at his elbow, placing a book before
him. When he glances down he sees that the book has

177

been opened, and that a marker has been placed in it. His eye seeks the appropriate passage: 'A virtuous woman who can find? Her price is above rubies.' At some further point he is aware of Lautner cutting at the lapel of his jacket, rending his garment.

Alfred stands all night in his mother's room, at the foot of her bed. I never meant to leave you, he says, and now he knows it to be true.

F O U R T E E N

W REN HOUSE is sold. To be honest, nobody misses it.
Muriel has been returned to her brother's bunga-
low, holding herself in readiness for a sign from Alfred
that he has bought another house and will require her
services once more. The acquisition of this house is becoming illusory, in the manner of Alfred's other projects. He
is constantly on the point of moving out of Bryanston
Square, selling the firm, going to live abroad, buying an
estate in Herefordshire, putting money into a stud farm,
settling in Scotland. He may be going to do any or all of
these things but he will certainly have to do something:
now that Mimi and Lautner have moved back to Bryanston Square Alfred's temper is constantly on the boil,
although the meals are the meals he always loved as a boy,
and both Mimi and Lautner beam with pleasure when he
joins them in the drawing-room. But it is a dreary life, he
thinks, moving from his study to his bedroom; con-
venient but dreary. When he has decided whether it is to
be Scotland or Herefordshire, winter quarters in Madeira
or a service flat in Whitehall Court, he will soon be gone.
Once he has arranged for the firm to be liquidated and the
money to be suitably invested, then he will be a free man
at last. Yet he seems not to be in a hurry to implement
any of these plans. Something keeps him in Bryanston
Square, some factor in his life which says, Stay. As if it

were a voice which, when he becomes impatient and begins to rage as he did as a boy, says, Stay. Thus, for the time being, he remains at Bryanston Square.

He never ran away with Dolly. Somehow the idea disappeared when his mother died. Although the scrupulous Hal remained impassive and courteous, although Dolly herself became more openly possessive, the idea of Dolly, as opposed to the reality, seemed to change overnight from alluring to distasteful. Alfred, who previously thrilled to the evidences of Dolly's impudence, began to see that they were in fact tiresome. He began to see that the management of Dolly was in fact entirely in the hands of Hal, and that without the assurance of Hal's massive patience Dolly could quite quickly go off the rails. What form this would take was not quite clear but Alfred, a bachelor, has always been uneasy about female tantrums. He probably has some memory trace of his sister Betty as a child, screaming herself red in the face, tears spurting from her eyes, only to be comforted by Frederick, ever indulgent to a woman even if that woman were only his sister. It is curious how easily Alfred appears to have come to terms with what others might see as quite a major defeat. But it was in fact Alfred who proposed that they should go on that Mediterranean cruise together, all five of them: Dolly and Hal, Nettie and Will, and himself, the generous host. He said that he was grateful to them for rallying round during his mother's last days, and indeed family feeling seems to be growing in him at last. The cruise, during which Dolly wore a great deal of white linen and got rather drunk in the evenings, and Nettie's still red hair shone like a marigold in the fierce sun, and Hal and Will settled down amicably in deck-chairs with a cigar and a couple of good political biographies, found Alfred at last reconciled to foreign shores. Leaning on the guardrail, surveying the next port of call, he appeared to reflect that compromise is not a bad solution, and that modified escape does not destroy the possibility of return. The cruise was a great success and has been repeated every spring for the past five years.

Mimi lost her baby. They put it down to shock at her mother's death, and, sadly, it was clear that she would never have another. For a long time she was quite ill, sliding back into that depression, that irradiation of the spirit, that had afflicted her so long ago on her return from Paris. There is a period in her life which was almost entirely unlived. When Lautner came home in the evenings he would find her lying on the sofa, as he had left her that morning, looking to him as if she had not moved from that moment to this. Mimi would be quite unable to say what she had done with her day. All she could remember was lying on the sofa, listening to the pneumatic drills in the road outside: the sun, a hot white disk, seemed blurred and obscured by the dust rising from the pavement. No breeze stirred the long stiff lace curtains and the green plants looked fleshy and venomous in their Indian brass pots. All day long Mimi lay there, looking at the blighted sun, hearing the shattering drills, until she almost ceased to be aware of where she was or why she was there. It was Alfred, exasperated as he always was by Mimi's languishing condition, who suggested that Lautner and she move back to Bryanston Square. 'It is the most sensible idea,' he said. 'She will be happier there. And in any event the place will soon be yours. As soon as I have settled my affairs I shall be gone.'

For Mimi, coming home was a sort of completion, perhaps the only one possible after that original false start and her recent tragedy. If Mimi's cup ever runneth over, it runneth over with decency rather than with anything more vital. Since losing the baby she has become very much more dependent on Lautner, who is indeed a devoted husband. See how patriarchally he places encompassing arms on the back of the sofa on which Mimi is seated! See how he stands when she enters the room and opens the door when she leaves it! Mimi accepts these attentions gratefully and graciously. She seems to have abandoned her determination to be a young matron and is now actively training to be an older one. She glides about the apartment with an ever watchful eye to its good management: sweet smells of lavender and vetiver issue from her cupboards, and the journals are all uncreased on the table in the study. This is perhaps her true apotheosis, this return to the still intact dreams of her girlhood. If occasionally a sigh escapes her it is because she sees now how it could and should have been. But all that is past now and she can take pride in the well-regulated life that she always knew she was called upon to live. The piano is silent these days. Since the loss of her baby Mimi finds that music upsets her, brings on a headache. She finds too that these headaches can only be relieved by slow relentless tears. For this reason she has decided to get rid of the piano, although Lautner is sad about this. The piano played a large part in his life and he would be sorry to see it go. But Mimi, straight backed in one of those muted silk dresses in which she so resembles her mother, has no time now for Lautner's sentimentality. She knows exactly how like a lingering illness sentiment can be, and how effectively it can interfere with one's duties.

Sometimes Mimi gets up from the sofa and goes to the window. Not very often because she does not allow herself too much time for day-dreaming, and in any event since Lili's marriage she only has Ursie in the kitchen to help her. Sometimes Mimi thinks, if only I had been bolder, had tried again sooner, had pushed my claims. But she never thought she had any claims, had only waited, and, waiting, had been found. And, after all,

honour has been saved. She has married, she has con-
ceived. And if the outcome has not been all that she had
wished, well, that is occasionally the way with outcomes.
And there was always this suspicion, born when she sat
at the piano in Mr Cariani's academy and heard Betty
stamping away at her dancing, that the good live unhappily ever after.

Nothing much is heard from the others these days.
When Sofka died, Frederick and Evie sent a telegram:
'Heartbroken. Thinking of her today and every day.'
Occasionally Evie writes, long enthusiastic empty letters
in her flowing script, lavish with endearments and promises of a visit home as soon as they have appointed a new
manager or overseen the last stage of the redecoration,
but nothing ever seems to come of these reassurances. It
is always Evie who writes these letters: Frederick appears
to have dematerialized into the Riviera sun. Alfred telephoned him from Marseilles when the ship made a stop
there, but Frederick was not in and Evie could not be
found. Perhaps Frederick was in Nice, at the Ruhl, pursuing his afternoon ritual, still with that ceremonious grace
that now appears so old-fashioned. Frederick does not
know this, or if he knows does not care. His instincts
have served him so well all his life that it would be disloyal
of him to abandon them. And so, portly now, but light
on his feet, Frederick lifts his hat to ladies young and old
in the streets of Bordighera and raises a glass smilingly to
his wife at dinner. His children, rangy French-looking
teenagers who have grown out of their resemblance to
their mother, will shortly leave home and be seen only
intermittently, in the holidays. The rest of the time they
will speed about Europe fearlessly on their mopeds and
plan to settle in America as soon as they are old enough.

Betty too is plumper, older. Looking after Max has
condemned her to a sedentary life, and she always had a

sweet tooth. These days she sits beside the pool, tightly encased in the latest beachwear, her hair dyed a vivid red, her mouth an enlarged scarlet bow. Betty has not moved with the times, although she occasionally attempts to get her figure back with yoga exercises. Most of her days are spent watching television, old films which give Max pleasure. She prepares little snacks for him, little Hollywood salads of cottage cheese and fruit, little confections of pineapple and coconut. She thinks it shameful of Alfred not to send more money, but this is an old grudge and one that no longer corresponds with the truth. The money arrives regularly but Betty is still apt to flare up when she thinks of Mimi in Bryanston Square. It has been suggested to her by Max that she should go home for a visit, but they both know what this means. It means that if and when Max dies Betty will have to go back and live with her brother and sister. This knowledge is rejected. Betty shudders delicately when the subject is mentioned. 'That awful weather,' she grimaces. 'My health would never stand it.' For she knows that she will never go home again and that some old trouper's pride will keep her sitting here, by the pool, to the very end.

What happened to the ludic impulse that was once so strong in Frederick and in Betty? Although it seems that Mimi, with awful dignity, has at last and finally acknowledged that her life is to be lived without it, how can it be that Frederick is content to spend his days as an ageing hotelier, in a resort that none but the retired are now prone to visit, with only the minute distraction of his afternoons at the Ruhl to compensate him? Why does Betty, so fiery and so fearless in her early days, sit like a child, in her childlike clothes, eating concoctions that might have been devised for a child's party? Can it be that their youthful habits pertained only to their youth, and that middle age has left them stranded, without guidelines, and curiously and noticeably devoid of impetus? Can it be that the presence of a partner, who can be said, in both cases, to be the ideal partner, has somehow subsumed the essence of those who once appeared so strong, so self-aware? Who could have foretold the ulti-mate passivity of Frederick and of Betty, subsiding into the permanence of what was originally a temporary arrangement, with a backward glance only to the mythic elements of their own lives? How have these artists in self-referral managed to edit themselves into a version so static, and yet so emblematic, that those at home, who have not seen them for many years, have no difficulty at all in picturing them, Frederick in his linen jacket and his panama hat and his pale shoes, smiling and strolling and savouring his pleasures, the boulevardier of his mother's imagination, and Betty, cross-grained and vivid in her flimsy clothes, eternally toying with something coloured in a long glass, and glancing down critically at her painted toenails? Can it be that the ludic impulse, once so strong, has vanished, or has transmuted, or transferred, leaving those early celebrants adrift, becalmed, yet somehow legendary?

These thoughts frequently occur to Mimi, who has always pondered more deeply than any of the others. She reflects on the pluses and minuses of life to a quite considerable extent these days, and the thinking has hol-lowed her cheeks, made her stately, rather handsome, yet not too communicative. Mimi has acquired depth, a depth not of her own choosing. She is mildly matriarchal, given to sober pursuits, an excellent housewife. She is at ease with Lautner and his elderly ways, no longer seeking diversion. They still take their afternoon walks, for Lautner, now retired, is tireless in his self-appointed task of supervising Mimi's health and comfort. They talk little of those matters which they both still have at heart, managing to convert their memories into a pleasant concern for each other's welfare, and relying on the habits of a lifetime to see them through certain dark moments. In this they are successful. They are to be found in the drawing-room, with a silver tray of coffee-cups in front of them, entertaining visitors, family and friends. They drive out with Alfred to see those various properties which he has not so far decided to buy, but which he surely will some day, one day. And it is Mimi the matriarch and Alfred the man of property that Frederick and Betty idly or resentfully envisage when they turn their thoughts to home from their sunlit exile.

But what Frederick and Betty signally fail to envisage is the transmutation of their own early singularity, of that wild card that, in their hands, was to take them so far away, and then to leave them, stranded. Nobody knows what has happened to that wild card. Nobody talks about it. But nobody thinks of it as being entirely absent, or unable to recur.

To all intents and purposes life changes very little in Bryanston Square. Alfred is still there, although he has his eye on a house on the Suffolk coast. One of these days he will run Mimi down to see it. Until then, or until he thinks of another house, somewhere else, the time passes without their noticing it very much. On most evenings they have visitors. Dolly and Hal come, although Dolly is so discontented these days that she needs a great deal of cajoling; in the middle of a conversation she is apt to announce, 'I want another brandy.' Hal purses his lips. This is becoming a problem, although he supposes that he can deal with it. Lili and Benjie bring their two enchanting children, Laurie (Laura) and Charlie (Charles, but in reality Karl, after Lili's dead father). Mrs Beck, who has remained in touch with both Mimi and the girls, still enters the room with a faintly admonitory air but gets on very well with Lautner who is now quite old. They have much in common, these two. Lautner introduced young George Beck into the firm of Dorn and Co. and is always delighted to know how he is getting on. It has long been hoped that George would marry Ursie, who has been a little bit short-tempered since her sister left. But she is a good girl, though no longer quite so pretty; she has always liked George, and, more important, Mrs Beck, and now it seems certain that she will settle down. They are all so pleased. Will and Nettie come, with their little daughter, for the unexpected happened, just when it seemed to be almost too late: a child, after all these years. It seemed like a miracle, and perhaps it was. Mimi smiles, serves coffee, serves marzipan cake.

Here they all are, family and friends, in the wedding photograph. It is the last one in the album. George and Ursie stand, politely smiling, between Lili and Mrs Beck. Dolly, slightly out of focus, as she was in reality on that day, appears to lean heavily on Hal. Will smiles, plump, good-natured, unquestioning as ever. Mimi, upright, in pale lace, with a rather imposing hat, looks very like her mother. Lautner, although greatly diminished, still turns to her fondly. Here is Alfred, tall, stiff, still a handsome man. Here is Nettie, very close to Alfred, leaving Will almost unattached, unpaired. And in the front row, the three children: Laurie, Charlie, and Nettie's child Vicky (Victoria). See that look on Vicky's face, that imperious stare, so unlike a child, so like Sofka. See Alfred's hand proudly clasping her little shoulder. See the resemblance. Wait for the dancing to begin.

Anita Brookner, an international authority on eighteenth- and nineteenth-century art, teaches at the Courtauld Institute of Art in London. In 1968 she was Slade Professor at Cambridge, the first woman ever to hold this position. She is the author of *Watteau: The Genius of the Future; Greuze; Jacques-Louis David;* and of three earlier novels— *The Debut* (published in England as *A Start in Life*), *Look at Me, Providence,* and *Hotel du Lac.*